"Cal, whe
murmured.

His smile tore her heart to pieces. "You're too honest, my beautiful B.J. You shouldn't have said that, because now I'm not going to let you think. I'm only going to make you feel." He slid his fingers to her ear, traced the outline of it with just one, then moved and pressed it softly against that mad little pulse in her throat, and watched her eyes flare with shining violet lights. "What do you feel when I touch you like that?"

She lifted her gaze to meet his. "Warm. Tingly."

"Good. Because when I touch you, I feel hot. And throbbing."

She remembered their kisses, how they made her feel hot and throbbing too. She wanted those feelings now even though she was still afraid. And she wanted him as she'd never wanted anyone or anything in her life. B.J. looked at Cal, unable to disguise her longing.

Then he kissed her. It was nothing like any other kiss they had shared. This was a kiss from him that said, *here I am, take me,* to which she answered fervently, *me too,* with nothing more than her lips. In that moment, she knew she was lost. . . .

WHAT ARE *LOVESWEPT* ROMANCES?

They are stories of true romance and touching emotion. We believe those two very important ingredients are constants in our highly sensual and very believable stories in the *LOVESWEPT* line. Our goal is to give you, the reader, stories of consistently high quality that may sometimes make you laugh, sometimes make you cry, but are always fresh and creative and contain many delightful surprises within their pages.

Most romance fans read an enormous number of books. Those they truly love, they keep. Others may be traded with friends and soon forgotten. We hope that each *LOVESWEPT* romance will be a treasure—a "keeper." We will always try to publish

LOVE STORIES YOU'LL NEVER FORGET
BY AUTHORS YOU'LL ALWAYS REMEMBER

The Editors

LOVESWEPT® • 377
Judy Gill
Golden Swan

 BANTAM BOOKS
NEW YORK • TORONTO • LONDON • SYDNEY • AUCKLAND

GOLDEN SWAN

A Bantam Book / January 1990

LOVESWEPT® and the wave device are registered
trademarks of Bantam Books, a division of
Bantam Doubleday Dell Publishing Group, Inc.
Registered in U.S. Patent
and Trademark Office and elsewhere.

If you would be interested in receiving protective vinyl
covers for your Loveswept books, please write to this address
for information:

Loveswept
Bantam Books
P.O. Box 985
Hicksville, NY 11802

ISBN 0-553-44010-1

Published simultaneously in the United States and Canada

Bantam Books are published by Bantam Books, a division
of Bantam Doubleday Dell Publishing Group, Inc. Its trademark, consisting of the words "Bantam Books" and the
portrayal of a rooster, is Registered in U.S. Patent and
Trademark Office and in other countries. Marca Registrada.
Bantam Books, 666 Fifth Avenue, New York, New York 10103.

PRINTED IN THE UNITED STATES OF AMERICA

O   0 9 8 7 6 5 4 3 2 1

One

Cal sat up straighter in his chair and massaged the small of his back with both hands. The motion elicited an eager question from the younger of his two nieces, ten-year-old Kara. "Are you finished, Uncle Cal? Can we have a canoeing lesson now?"

"Soon," he said absently, and rotated his shoulders to get rid of the kinks. He hated paperwork. He hated government forms, but they had to be filled out every month his lodge was in operation. September, the closing month of the season, meant even more paperwork. He heard a long, gusty sigh behind him, followed by another. He, too, sighed as he turned to face the girls.

"I wish you two would quit sulking."

"We're not sulking," said Laura with all the injured dignity of an insulted eleven-year-old. "We may be feeling sad, but we never sulk."

He raised his brows and flashed them a quick grin. "You could have fooled me." Laura met his gaze with eyes most definitely sad. Kara stared at him, too, her mouth drooping.

"If you're so desperately unhappy here," Cal asked,

"why do I hear the two of you laughing and giggling and carrying on when you're in your room, or think I'm out of hearing range? You're only 'sad' when I'm around, so I can only conclude that you're sulking and trying to make me feel guilty for not inviting your great-aunt to come here with you."

"Is it working?" Kara asked with interest and some hope.

Cal suppressed a smile. "Nope," he said, and turned back to his paperwork.

"What if we told you that she's really young and beautiful?" Laura asked.

He laughed and hooked one arm over the back of his chair, turning back to the girls. "You never give up, do you? I'm not asking her here. This is no place for an old lady. She'd hate it."

"But—" Kara broke off and cocked her head to one side. "What's that?" They could all hear a whining motor, coming closer, growing louder.

Cal rose to his feet. "I don't know. It's not a plane, and it shouldn't be an outboard. Not on Kinikinik Lake." As a waterfowl preserve, the lake was supposed to be free of powerboats. Float planes, however, were permitted, but the noise certainly wasn't from one of those.

"It sounds like a motorcycle," Laura said, going to a window that looked up the valley through the orchard. "But how could there be one up here?"

"There are old logging roads that connect all the way out to Powell River," Cal said, shoving his feet into shoes as he looked out the window over Laura's head. There was nothing to see, but the machine was certainly approaching fast. "Maybe someone's lost and needs help," he continued, heading for the rear entrance. "Though during hunting season, nobody but a lunatic would be out on a motorcycle in the woods."

"Lunatic?" Laura echoed, crowding past her uncle. "Of course! A lunatic on a motorcycle! Kara, come on! It's B.J.!" she shrieked, tearing out the door. "Our letters worked!"

"What?" Cal followed their headlong rush outside. "B.J.? Who's B.J.? What the hell's going on and who in the hell is that and—*look out!*"

The last was a shout of warning as a motorcycle shot over the brow of the hill, hit the slick mud where Fred had recently cleaned out an irrigation ditch, and went into a skid. The rider righted the bike, jumped on the brakes, and cut the motor. Cal could see he was fighting the machine, dragging his feet, trying to slow it as it continued to slide through the mud. A low moan of horror came from under the visored helmet in the brief seconds before the bike crashed through the rear wall of the greenhouse.

It came to rest finally, wedged between the potting table and a support beam.

In the shocked silence glass tinkled musically. Cal stepped into the greenhouse and gingerly brushed broken bits of glass from the hunched shoulders of the leather-clad figure still astride the bike. A heartfelt "whew!" whispered out from the helmet.

From somewhere behind him, a small, scared voice asked, "B.J.? Are you okay?"

The girls seemed certain that the rider was the mysterious B.J., Cal thought as a pair of gauntleted hands released the handlebars and the leather-covered shoulders shrugged off his touch. The rider scrambled off the bike awkwardly, turned from the scene f destruction, and removed the visored helmet.

Shimmering blond hair tumbled around a stark white face. A pair of incredibly blue eyes gazed at Cal almost without seeing him, blinked, and focused on the girls.

"Hello, my angels," the woman said through bloodless lips, her voice thin but musical. "I got your letters. I came as soon as I could."

"What happened?" Kara asked. "Why did you crash?"

"The—the brakes locked." B.J. turned to look at the shattered wall of the greenhouse. Then, with a faint sigh, she keeled over to land with a thud, facedown among the hills of potatoes. Her helmet rolled over to Cal's feet, teetering there like a strange red bowl.

"B.J.!" Laura cried, flinging herself down beside the unconscious woman. "Oh, Uncle Cal, help her! She must be hurt. Pick her up or something!"

"Yeah. Sure. Pick her up—or something," he muttered, crouching at the woman's other side. Gently, he turned her onto her back and smoothed the hair off her forehead, feeling the silky strands slide through his fingers. When he brushed the dry soil of the potato bed off her face, he was aware of the satiny texture of her creamy skin, and felt guilty for noticing.

With infinite care, he ran his hands over the one-piece leather suit she wore. Even as he wondered if he'd recognize a life-threatening injury when he felt one, he was very much aware that injuries were not what he was most interested in. Her legs were slender, her hips flared with feminine grace, and her breasts were full and rounded. Her arms, when he forced his hands to tend to them, seemed intact, and she had been able to stand. She had spoken to the girls. He didn't really think she was hurt badly. The impact of her bike with the greenhouse hadn't been all that hard, her speed having been slowed by her boots dragging furrows in the garden. Still, he was careful as he slid his arms under her and lifted her limp form against his chest. She was light, yet there was a warm substance to her that made a solid impact on his senses. Something shuddered through him that had no right to be there, but he couldn't quite eradicate it.

He watched her for indications of discomfort as he moved her, but her face, though white, remained relaxed. He was deeply grateful she'd worn a visored helmet. It would have been a desecration if her face had been cut. Her face . . .

He swallowed again as he shifted her in his arms and stood up. Whoever she was, she had the most exquisite face he had ever seen. Her skin was like porcelain. No, alabaster. No, mother-of-pearl. Oh, what did it matter? It was perfection. Her lashes, dark and thick and luxuriant, lay in long sweeps below her eyes. Her eyes . . .

Had he imagined the blueness of them, the intensity of their color, the depths he had seen in just that one flashing instant?

"Is she dead?" Kara asked fearfully. Cal shook his head. "No. I think she's just passed out. Probably from fright. I guess skidding into a greenhouse on a bike with locked brakes isn't listed among life's most pleasant experiences."

As he spoke Cal carried the woman to the house, standing aside while Laura lunged forward to open the door. He sat down on the couch, still holding her. Unable to help himself, he stroked her face again, removing any remaining traces of garden soil, sensitive once more to the satiny texture of her skin.

"Wake up," he said gently, patting her cheek, watching color slowly return to tinge her cheeks and lips with pink. "Come on, beautiful. Wake up. Get a cold cloth, Laura. Kara, go look in the medicine cabinet in your bathroom. I think there's smelling salts in the first-aid kit.

"Wake up," he repeated as the girls hurried off. "Open your lovely eyes, Sleeping Beauty. You're safe

now, you know." She failed to respond beyond a
faint parting of her luscious lips, and a fluttering of
dark lashes. He stared at her mouth. No lipstick.
That rosy color was natural. He studied the rest of
her face. Again, no makeup. Completely natural.
And she was still the most incredibly beautiful woman
he had ever seen.

Impulsively, he bent his head and brushed his
lips over hers. If she could be Sleeping Beauty, why
couldn't he be Prince Charming and wake her with
a magic kiss?

Something in him quivered when her lips moved
gently under his. He felt her breath on his cheek,
smelled the sweet, fresh outdoors scent of her skin
and hair, and succumbed to the insistent demand
drumming within. His arms tightened around her.
He groaned softly, then parted her lips with his own
as they hardened over hers and kissed her more
deeply. She sighed into his mouth and her tongue
flicked almost shyly against his lower lip.

Astonished delight ran through him as her hand
came up and cupped his cheek, so soft and warm
and delicate, and her tongue tasted him again. . . .

B.J. heard a deep, resonant, male voice speaking
to her through a cloud of purple gauze. It was a
wonderful voice, a caring one, vibrant with concern.
The man's hand touched her face with callused fingertips, and that, too, was wonderful. She kept her
eyes closed, drifting in a wide, slow circle, and then
she felt the pressure of his mouth on hers.

Her heart stilled for an instant, then hammered
hard in her chest. Her throat tightened at the taste
of this man with the velvet voice. His arms were
stronger, yet gentler, than any arms that had held
her before. His chest was broader, harder, and the

warmth that emanated from his body reached right to her core, even through her leathers.

Leathers? Yes. She was wearing her biking clothes. Where was she? Why was she in this man's arms? Why had he told her to wake up? Had she fallen and knocked herself out? From somewhere came the knowledge that she shouldn't be enjoying this so much, that there was another reason for her having come here—wherever "here" might be—but if that was so, why did his kiss, though it tasted slightly odd, feel so right?

She had no answers to those questions, but it didn't matter, did it? What mattered was that this was happening and it was sensational and she didn't want it to end. She flicked her tongue out, wanting to taste him again, wondering what that intriguing flavor was, and heard the soft, explosive sound of his breath, felt the warmth of it against her cheek. She wanted to touch him, and touched him, because it was easier to give in to the desire than to struggle against it.

She was conscious, Cal realized as her hand slid around to the back of his head and clung to his hair. She was conscious, and she was kissing him back. She was participating equally in this heady, unbelievable delight, enjoying it with the same abandoned pleasure as he.

He groaned softly as he lifted her higher in his arms, feeling her soft hair caress his throat, her bottom nestle against his lap, the quickening rise and fall of her chest as her breathing became as tremulous as his own. She felt like heaven in his arms. She felt better than any other woman had ever felt. He wanted to hold her like this for the rest of his life, and he didn't even know who she was!

"Uncle Cal! What are you doing?"

Laura's shocked voice, as much as his own realization, brought him to attention and he abruptly lifted his mouth away from the woman's. What had he been doing? Even more important, what had he been thinking? Crazy thoughts, that was what! Stupid ones. Completely out-of-character ones.

"Um . . . I . . . Didn't you ever hear of mouth-to-mouth resuscitation?" he snapped, then tenderly settled the now fully conscious woman into the corner of the sofa. He arranged a plump pillow behind her head, then stood and swung her legs up to where he had been sitting. All the while he tried to avoid getting caught in the web she cast with the intense gaze of those blue, blue eyes. He couldn't avoid it. They were there, those eyes, calling to him, beckoning him. He looked, promising himself it would just be one tiny glance, that he couldn't be captured if he only looked for an instant. But they ensnared him, pinned him, gazing at him with an odd mixture of bewilderment, confusion, and . . . *yearning*? Could it be that she felt it, too? The wonder, the promise, the instant attraction he felt for her?

From a long way away he heard Laura say, "Oh. But . . . she wasn't drowned, Uncle Cal." The woman, still looking at him, blushed a lovely shade of pink, enchanting him further.

"I can't find anything that says 'smelling salts,' " Kara wailed from along the hall.

Suddenly those blue eyes smiled into his, offering to share amusement, making his head spin. In that melodious voice, stronger now, she called out . . . "Try 'sal volatile,' honey, but don't worry about it. I'm fine now and don't need smelling salts."

Because something better had come along to wake her up? Cal wondered. His heart pounded so hard, he thought it might not stay confined within his chest.

"Oh, B.J.!" Laura launched herself into B.J.'s arms to be joined by her smaller sister only seconds later. "You're here! You're really here! I can't believe it! When did you get our letters? You see, Uncle Cal? She really is young and beautiful! Oh, please say you don't mind! You'll let her stay now that she's here and you can see how really nice she is, won't you?"

Cal felt his knees grow watery as he sank onto the edge of a chair. He stared at the two girls wriggling in delight as they hugged and kissed the woman on the couch, the woman he wanted to hug and kiss, too. But if he joined that tangle of arms and legs and kisses, he'd wriggle in more than just delight. It was much, much better, he decided, to stay completely out of that—reunion?

"I don't believe this," he said, looking at the woman over the heads of his nieces. "You aren't . . . you can't be. You aren't trying to tell me that you're Melody's aunt Barbara? The girls' great-aunt? My God! You can't be!" he repeated. "You can't be *anyone's* great-anything!"

"But I am." She smiled at him. "I come from a weirdly spaced family. I have two brothers, ages fifty-seven and fifty-six, and one sister, Melody's mother, Phyllis, who's fifty-four. They were all grown—Phyllis was twenty-four—when I was born."

She smiled at him again and the world started spinning faster. She had dimples, adorable, trembling dimples, one on either side of her mouth. He knew he must look vacuous and inane, with his mouth hanging open while he grinned like a lunatic.

That reminded him. "The minute I said 'lunatic on a motorcycle,' Laura, you knew exactly who was out there. Why? How?"

B.J. laughed lightly and little bells rang in his ears, making him dizzy. "Because" she said, "that's what her dear father calls me every time he sees me on the bike."

"Are you?" The thought appalled him. "Do you ride dangerously?"

"No. I'm a very safe rider, today's incident notwithstanding." She smiled again and those cute dimples danced and winked. Cal knew he'd always been a sucker for dimples—he'd just never noticed it before.

B.J. watched as the girls' uncle Cal got up, took a step toward the couch, and tripped over an ottoman. He staggered three feet forward and fell into another chair. There he remained, his gaze pinned to her face with . . . could it be fascination?

B.J. stared back. What was the matter with him? He was gaping at her like a stunned fish, and she certainly hadn't expected what Melody called the "dolt reaction" from him, of all people. Other men, on other occasions, sure, but never him. Since her transformation, men had tended to take second and third looks, and once in a while even to stutter, especially if they'd known her before, but nobody had ever tripped over the furniture because of her. In the back of her mind, she heard Melody's voice: *Go on up there, B.J., and knock him right on his patookus.*

Well! Had she done that? For a moment she thought that maybe she had, but though it was a pleasing idea, it was so ludicrous she abandoned it. She hadn't knocked Calvin Mixall onto anything. He hadn't expected her, that was all, and she must be a bit of a shock to him because she didn't look like a typical great-aunt. Most people were startled by the relationship.

"Uh—" He swallowed visibly. "Welcome to Kinikinik Lake, Miss Gray."

She smiled. "Thank you," she said, and to his delight, blushed again. "But please, won't you call me B.J. . . . Cal?"

Cal experienced a surge of desire in response to that alluring smile, then tried to negate its effect by returning it, but his didn't seem to do to her what hers did to him. She simply looked down, hiding her eyes with those thick dark lashes, and his insides flipped over. Dammit, he had to get himself together. This was insane! She was a woman, for heaven's sake. He'd seen plenty of women before. He'd held plenty of women before. Kissed them. *But not recently,* a little voice inside him said, and he heard it with relief.

All right, so that was it. That explained the whole incredible sequence of events, from his running his hands over her slender body while he thought of things other than broken bones, to his lifting her up into his arms and carrying her into his house with such a feeling of . . . Hell, he couldn't put a name to that particular feeling, but it was the most primitive emotion he'd ever experienced and had a lot to do with caves and fires and the warmth of animal skins. Possession.

"Please, Uncle Cal?" Kara wheedled. "She can stay, can't she? Now that she's here? I mean, when the school burned down, it was like her own house did, and she has no place to go since our house is being remodeled."

"Kara, honey, that's not quite true," B.J. said. "I have lots of friends I can stay with while the school's being rebuilt. In fact, I'm house-sitting for one right now while he's away on business."

Cal nearly groaned. He didn't doubt for a minute that the rest of those "friends" she could stay with were male, too. Hell, there was probably a long line of men begging her to use their spare room—or whatever.

"I only came for a day or two," B.J. went on, "just to see how you were settling in." And, she added silently, to make sure you weren't really being mistreated by the ogre you so dramatically painted for me in your last letter. "I'd like to get back on Saturday."

"Oh, no!" Kara wailed.

Laura added her two bits' worth. "But this is Thursday and that's not long enough. Uncle Cal, please, please tell her she can stay longer!"

He cleared his throat and smiled at Laura, then shrugged, giving in all at once. All at once? Hell! Even before he knew that B.J. was Great-Aunt Barbara, he'd wanted her to stay. But if she thought it was for the kids' sake, maybe it would look better. "Okay, sweetheart. It really is important to you girls, having your aunt here, isn't it?" he said with almost true contrition. "I'm sorry. I should have realized. Of course, B.J.'s welcome to stay for as long as she wants." Lord, he thought. Did his smile look as fatuous as it felt?

"Oh, Uncle Cal! Thank you! Thank you so much!"

Laura beamed and he added gruffly, "Just don't get the idea that I've given in because of your sulking."

"We won't, Uncle Cal!" Kara flew to him and perched on his lap, kissing his face over and over, saying, "Thank you, thank you, thank you! Oh, I do love you a lot!"

"I love you, too, punkin," he said, hugging her tightly.

Watching, B.J. thought he looked out of his depth and slightly bemused. For an ogre, that was. Her doubts as to that were growing ever stronger, along with doubts about other things as well.

Cal watched a series of expressions cross B.J.'s lovely, mobile face, saw her color come and go . . . and stay away as she briefly closed her eyes. He stood, carefully spilling Kara from his lap, and said, "Hey, you two, how 'bout you come out to the kitchen with me and help make B.J. some . . . tea or something."

"Not tea," Laura said. "B.J. drinks coffee."

"Okay, you can help me make coffee. You know how useless I am in the kitchen. We'll let your aunt rest for a few minutes."

B.J. was about to protest that she didn't need to rest, but he had grabbed both the girls by the hand and was leading them out. With a sigh, B.J. leaned back on the pillow he'd stuffed behind her. She didn't need to rest, but she sure as heck needed a few minutes to think. Assuming she could get her head on straight in the aftermath of those incredible kisses.

She hadn't expected that she'd react to his more than potent kiss the way she had. Of course, she hadn't expected to be kissed, but once she'd realized who the kisser was, she shouldn't have gone on responding the way she had. Dammit, long ago she had despised him, then had managed to forget him. Well, more or less. And she had to keep it that way, she remembered with a shock of realization. Where had her good sense gone in those short moments while their lips were joined, moving over and under each other's, tasting, testing, searching? Sense. It was something she'd have to hang on to very tightly, because she'd been attracted to this man once, and it was not going to happen again!

She had flatly refused Melody's frantic request a couple of weeks ago that she go to the girls' "rescue," as her niece and dear friend had so dramatically put it. That phone call, on the eve of Mel and her husband Curtis's departure for Asia, had triggered too many unhappy memories, had opened up old hurts and long-forgotten feelings of humiliation. She wanted only to hide her head and pretend none of it had ever happened.

But it had happened and she had never really been able to let go of the stinging shame she had felt. Melody didn't know what Cal had done that weekend, but had advised B.J. to forget it.

"Let the past go, B.J. Cal's not the same guy you met twelve and a half years ago. He's grown up. He's a wonderful man. Do you think I'd entrust the girls to him if he weren't? And since you and Cal are their joint guardians while Curtis and I are away, why not?"

"Because I can't even deal with thinking about your brother-in-law. And if I can't cope with memories, how could I cope with meeting the man again face-to-face?"

"But he's not the same man! B.J., come on, be sensible. You never told me what he did to annoy you so much, but how important can it be now? That was over twelve years ago."

B.J. wasn't about to tell Melody even now. But the fact remained, Calvin Mixall had not "annoyed" her. He had devastated her and she couldn't forgive him. "I never want to see him again."

"He's changed, I tell you." Indeed, Melody had told her, ad nauseam, over the past two years just how much her brother-in-law had changed. He was, according to Mel, far more interested in birds and animals than in women. He spent nearly half his time tucked away in a little corner of the wilderness, painting.

"And so have you changed," Melody reminded her.

That, B.J. was forced to admit, was true. Gloriously, unbelievably true. Who would have thought that losing a pile of weight and having her nose fixed would have made such a difference?

"If he's changed so much," she asked Melody, "that he's become a virtual recluse, then why did he agree to my going up there?"

"He . . . uh, doesn't know you're coming."

"What do you mean, he doesn't know I'm coming?

I wouldn't even consider going up there unless he had agreed to it! Which is more than I've done, Mel."

"Oh, but you have to, B.J.," Melody said cajolingly. "The girls need a woman with them, and they'd have been with you if your stupid school hadn't burned down at the last minute. I know Cal's family, too, but frankly, the girls need more than just a couple of old bachelors for company."

B.J. said nothing, and Mel went on with a light laugh, "Not that Cal's by any means old, of course, as I'm sure you remember. And if you just arrive, since you're the girls' coguardian, what can he say? I mean, it's not as though there wouldn't be room for you. The place is enormous, and there are no guests at this time of year. Heavens, he'll probably welcome you with open arms and—"

"Mel, stop it! I don't trust you. You've been trying to fix me up with your precious brother-in-law for the past two years, ever since he moved out here to the coast. I can't. Really, I can't."

"B.J., darling, when are you going to gain the confidence you should have at your age, and with your looks? You are a very beautiful woman and you can hold your own with anybody."

Maybe with anyone else, but *not* with Calvin Mixall, B.J. thought. Of course, Melody was right. She shouldn't feel so defensive, so awkward, but she did. And there was nothing to be done about it. If she saw Melody's brother-in-law again, the one who'd hurt her so deeply, she'd revert to the same puddle of suffering. Even now she could hear his raucous laughter—at her expense. Lord! The words spoken by his friend that she'd overheard as she shamelessly eavesdropped had nearly killed her. . . .*thought you might be expecting a flood, the way you've been clinging all evening to that big orange life raft . . .* She had known at once who the man referred to as she stood behind the screen in her horrid orange dress, the only thing she had been able to find that fit her three-hundred-pound figure half decently. It hadn't been the other man's words, though, but the sound of Cal's laughter that had rung in her nightmares for weeks after.

How could she tell Melody that the hurt and humiliation had gone so deep because she had thought that for once a man had seen beneath the surface and had liked the girl who lived hidden within the ugly body, behind the hideous, acne-pocked face? Melody had never looked like B.J. She couldn't possibly understand.

"I can't explain it," she said to Melody, "but even thinking about the man makes me feel . . . like *that* again."

"Well, you aren't 'like that.' Believe me, when he sees you, he won't remember you at all. He won't remember a thing! Hey, look at it this way, B.J. Why not go up there, bowl the poor guy over, knock him on his patookus, and then remind him of when you first met? Can you imagine his surprise?"

B.J. could. All too well. It would be a repeat of her meetings with other old male friends of the family. There had been too many insults in the past for her to warm up to any man who had known her and scorned her way back when. Men who couldn't see why she turned them down when they said things like, "Of course I always liked you—as a person—but really, how could I have asked you out? You understand."

Indeed, she did understand. What they didn't seem to understand was that their words, meant to be complimentary, hurt just as much as their former rejection.

"And anyway," she continued, "if I were to go way up there into the wilds with the kids, who'd be here to oversee the renovations to the house?"

"It's not exactly the wilds, B.J. It's only thirty or forty miles as the crow flies from Powell River."

"I'm not a crow, and I can't fly, and anyplace that takes two ferry trips to get to from Vancouver is in the wilds. No, Melody, it's out of the question."

"Cal has a plane, B.J. He could fly you out once a week or so to check on the renovations, and they'll be finished in a couple of months, anyway."

"In a couple of months the school will probably be back in operation, too, and the girls down here with me. So again, I say no. Absolutely not. Good-bye, Mel, darling. Have a wonderful time, and don't worry. The kids will be fine, bachelor uncle notwithstanding."

But when the girls' second letter came, with its pleadings, and then the third one, with its laments, it was the thought of those two darling kids left at the mercy of a heartless man that had decided her. Once decided, she had moved swiftly.

No point in giving him any warning by requesting a flight in, she'd told herself. Maps showed that there were roads, even if they were just logging roads, running right to the shores of Kinikinik Lake. If logging trucks could use them, then so could she, on her trail bike, and here she was.

And now . . . She wanted to laugh again. And now her nemesis, the former tormentor of her nightmares, had failed utterly to recognize her—just as Melody had predicted. He had called her beautiful. He had kissed her as if he had never wanted to stop, and she had felt his desire for her growing hard and urgent even though he'd tried to restrain himself.

He wanted her. This time he wanted her. This time he thought she was beautiful. And she found the knowledge exhilarating. It was the headiest feeling she had ever experienced. But, she thought, looking up as he came through the door bearing a tray of coffee, it was also scary. Too scary. She should run away very, very quickly because she wasn't used to feelings like this and didn't know if she could handle them. While her outside might have changed, deep within, she was still the same uncertain person, filled with fears and insecurities. Nothing in her life to date had equipped her to deal with a man like Calvin Mixall, even a Calvin Mixall who gazed at her as if she were dinner on the half shell. Especially him. He was an artist and would soon see through the sham that she was, and more than anything, she didn't ever want to hear his laughter at her expense again.

Two

"It's all decided, B.J.," Kara said, curling up beside her feet. "Uncle Cal wants you to stay here, too, so please say you will."

B.J. shook her head, smiling at Cal as he set the tray on the coffee table. She accepted the cup he offered her, lifting it high so that Laura could scoot under her arm and sit beside her, too.

"It'll be so much more fun with you here," Laura said, "and you can help us with our lessons and—"

"I've already said I can't stay long." She sipped awkwardly. "I could manage, though, until the end of the weekend, maybe Monday morning, but only if you guys move and let me sit up before your uncle kicks me out for putting my boots on his furniture." As the girls shifted out of her way, she sat up straight, swinging her feet to the floor. That was better. She could drink without risk of dribbling coffee down her chin.

"I was the one who put your boots on the furniture," Cal said. "Put your feet back up. Lie down. Are you sure you're feeling well enough to sit up?" He didn't know what he'd do if she passed out cold again. He'd have to pick her up. He'd have to hold her in his arms. He'd have to . . . have to what? There were children present! Innocent little girls! He had to get a grip on himself.

"I'm fine," she assured him, setting her cup on the table and lifting a hand to grasp the tab of her zipper.

She had beautiful fingernails, he noticed, filed to smooth, oval tips and painted pale pink. He could almost feel them raking down— He shivered and squeezed his eyes shut, but the sound of her zipper in motion had him staring again. She slid it down and he knew he was waiting, wondering. . . . Was his tongue hanging out? He sat down abruptly, hearing but not comprehending the chatter of the girls, B.J.'s replies, aware only of the sight of her figure being slowly unwrapped. . . .

Knock it off, Mixall! he wanted to shout. Instead, he eased his taut body back into the overstuffed chair and crossed his legs, trying to appear relaxed as the zipper continued down and down and down. The sides of the leather jumpsuit parted, revealing a soft pink sweater and the waistband of a pair of black . . . somethings. Pants. Of course, pants. He breathed again.

And stopped when she leaned forward to shrug out of the top half of the leather suit. Oh, yes, those breasts were as full as he'd imagined, the waist as tiny, the hips as flaring. She toed off her boots, then stood and skinned the leathers down her smooth, curving thighs. Under them she wore a pair of those pants he'd always thought looked painted on—and slightly obscene. The style, he knew now, had been invented with B.J. Gray in mind. The shiny black fabric clung to her skin—it could have been her skin—and it was driving him up the wall just to look at her . . . and not touch.

". . . right, Uncle Cal? Uncle Cal?" Laura reached over and poked him in the shoulder.

"Huh?" He blinked and stared at the child.

"You're going to teach us how to canoe, aren't you? When you have time."

"Oh. Oh, yes," he said absently. B.J. moved and his gaze swung up, drawn inexorably back to her as again the presence of the girls faded to nothing.

As if aware of his scrutiny, she looked at him, going very still. She didn't smile one of those incredible smiles, but still managed to cast the same spell over him, tightening the net imperceptibly. For one golden moment it was as if the two of them were all alone, wrapped in some kind of force field that kept the sounds and sights of the world away from them. Slowly, a flush rose in her cheeks, tinting them the same shade as her sweater. Her fingers tightened on her leather suit and her breathing was unsteady, lifting her breasts in tiny, jerking movements. She caught her lower lip between her teeth and looked down, her dark lashes fluttering maddeningly. Damn! he thought. She was an outrageous flirt and he usually shunned them, but he didn't want to shun her. He swallowed hard and then turned, as she did, to the sound of a door thudding open.

B.J. watched as the swinging doors to the kitchen parted with a *whoosh* and an elderly man come to a halt just inside the huge living room. He planted his muddy boots at the edge of the carpet, and faded blue eyes disappeared as his glasses fogged up. He took off the cloudy spectacles and squinted nearsightedly, hauling the tail of a grubby shirt out of baggy jeans to polish away the steam.

"Hey, boss! You know what? There's a gol-durned motorsickle right through the end of the gol-durned greenhouse! Where in the hell do you think that came from?"

B.J. stepped forward. "I'm afraid it's mine," she

said, intensely glad of the interruption. She had been in danger of losing herself in Cal Mixall's eyes, and that was the last place in the world she wanted to get lost.

The elderly man shoved his glasses back onto his big nose and stared at her.

"Yours?" he asked, incredulous. "Ladies drive motorsickles?"

She nodded.

He looked at her consideringly. Cal recognized the look. He'd known for some time that Fred was hoping to find himself a hardy lady who'd fit in here at Kinikinik Lake. He examined all the single ladies—and maybe some not so single—who came to go on hiking tours or canoe trips. The last Elderhostel group he'd hosted had kept Fred hopping with interest, but nothing had come of any of his attempts. Cal was sure the old goat was thinking that a lady who rode a motorbike had potential, even one clearly thirty or forty years too young.

"Miss Gray," Cal said quickly, moving to stand close to her, "meet Fred Carmody, the caretaker here. Fred, this is Barbara Gray."

Fred took off his glasses once more, cleaned them vigorously again, and put them on to peer more closely at B.J. "Pleased to meetcha, Miss Gray. Want me to bring your stuff in?"

"Call me B.J.," she said, and Cal felt something nasty uncurl inside him. She had used exactly the same phrase to him, and in exactly the same tone of voice. He wished he could see her face. Was she smiling that same kind of enchanting smile at Fred? Couldn't she see how old the old goat was?

"And thanks for your offer," she continued, "but I can get my bags myself. I don't want to be a bother, and I've caused enough trouble anyway, breaking the greenhouse. My insurance will cover the damage, of course."

"Don't be sil—" Cal began, but Fred interrupted him.

"No, no! There's no need for that. I can fix the greenhouse and gardening's all but finished for the season. It may only be September, but we'll be gettin' frosty nights soon. Winter comes early in the mountains. I'll carry your things in." Clearly, he was out to impress Cal's guest. Dammit, Cal thought, Fred had better remember exactly whose guest B.J. was, or he'd be reminded. Forcibly.

"Thank you, Fred," B.J. said, submitting gracefully.

Fred went back out through his trail of mud, leaving it even muddier, and leaving Cal's thoughts even bleaker. He could have carried her stuff in, for Pete's sake.

"Uncle Cal, where can B.J. sleep?" Laura asked, gathering up B.J.'s leathers. "Can she have the room that shares the bath with ours?"

Cal stood very still, resisting the urge to tell the girls to usher her right into his room. He wouldn't mind sharing a bath with her, or a shower, or . . . He shook his head quickly to disperse those fantasies, then nodded. "Sure, that sounds fine." Something made him follow the girls and their relative into the bedroom wing where they slept.

"Did you know there are fifteen bedrooms in this house?" Laura asked B.J. as she pushed open the door to the room they had chosen for her.

"That's because it was built to be a hunting lodge," Kara said. "Even though Uncle Cal only lets camera hunters come here now. I hope you'll like it," she added worriedly. "The rooms are sort of . . . Mom called them Spartan."

"That's because hunters, even camera hunters, don't spend a lot of time in their rooms," Laura said.

"Spartan doesn't bother me," B.J. said, gazing around the comfortably furnished room. There was a double bed, spread and curtains made to match, and a basic dresser with a mirror over it that reflected an oil painting on the opposite wall. She turned to look at it. It must be one of Cal's, she thought, wanting to examine it more closely even as she looked back at the girls. "Remember, I've lived and taught in a boarding school for the past three years, and opulence isn't considered necessary in teachers' quarters. Just being with you two for a few days is going to be great."

Kara hugged her tightly. "I'm so happy you came," she said. A lump rose in Cal's throat as he watched B.J. draw both the girls closer to her, her golden head bent to their dark ones.

"I know you miss your mom and dad," she said, "but just think of what a wonderful opportunity this is for them. Nepal, Tibet, India, Pakistan . . . It's something they've wanted to do for years. And think of the beautiful artworks they'll be bringing back for the stores!"

Curtis and Melody ran a chain of specialty shops that concentrated largely on Oriental art objects.

"And speaking of artworks," she went on, smiling at Cal as she indicated the painting. "Is this one of yours?"

He nodded, watching her as she looked in appreciation at his work. It made him feel warm all over that she liked it. He could tell by her face that she did. It didn't take her delighted laughter or her words, "It's great! What a marvelous expression you've captured," to convince him, and he felt like a winner in the warmth of her approval.

No matter what her personal opinion of the artist might have been, B.J. genuinely liked the oil painting. It was a study of a graceful white bird with one wing half-extended, its neck twisted around as it cleaned its feathers. On its face was an amusing expression of almost human disgruntlement. Clearly, it had not liked being disturbed during its preening activities.

This was the kind of work Cal Mixall was renowned for; the reality he captured, the soul of every animal he painted revealed. It had been written that Cal Mixall's paintings had done more to raise the consciousness of the average person and promote conversation than any other living artist. She had never been able to reconcile the man she remembered with the one who was so popular with columnists and interviewers for public affairs programs, but she had never really tried. She frowned, looking again at the picture.

Had she, all these years, hated someone who truly did not exist? Was the present-day Cal Mixall the man she should be looking at, not the one she remembered? She turned to say something to him, but he was gone. Just like that, without a word, he had slipped away. She wondered why.

Cal sat on a hard chair in the kitchen, his chin in his hands, trying to breathe deeply and steadily, trying to fight down the desire that B.J. Gray's smile, her laughter, even her appreciation of his work, had engendered in him. This was utter madness! Dammit, he wasn't ready for this. He didn't want it. He wanted peace, time to paint, to prepare for that damned pre-Christmas sale and exhibit he'd promised to be ready for, and here he was sitting on his butt, in a sweat because a woman had smiled at him! What the hell had gotten into him? Dammit, if Melody had planned this, she couldn't have found someone better qualified to shoot down his fierce independence and . . .

Holy mackerel! He sat up straight, mouth dropping open. Had she? Of course. He slumped again. He could see it now. He *had* been set up. And not only had Melody set him up, his own brother had been in on it, too! For a brief, crazy moment, he wondered if one of them had torched the boarding school.

Melody . . . He remembered the way she had tried to manipulate him. . . .

At dinner her last night there, she had stared at him speculatively, then smiled a distinctly feline smile. "Yes," she said. "That's the answer."

"Answer to what?"

"Barbara," she said, and turned to her husband. "We'll ask Barbara to come and help Cal with the girls, since he doesn't want a stranger." Her smile turned into a grin. "She'll be *such* a help."

Curt's eyes widened. "B-Barbara?" He coughed explosively. "Do you mean—"

"That's right, my aunt Barbara," Melody interrupted, pounding her husband on the back. "The girls' great-aunt," she added, transferring her smile to Cal, as if he weren't capable of figuring out the relationship himself. "Your coguardian."

"The *teacher*? Hell, Melody, what are you thinking of? An old lady here? No way!"

"No?" Melody said mildly. She shrugged. "I was only trying to help, to come up with a good idea, but if you say no . . ." She smiled again. "Never mind. You'll be meeting her when you take the girls out once the school is finished."

"Why is it so important that I meet her?"

"I guess it's not, but I was only thinking she should be here to share the responsibilities with you."

"I can manage the responsib—"

Cal broke off, scowling down into the empty glass in his hand. He was remembering the box of supplies Melody had tucked away into the girls' bathroom. After drawing his attention to it, she'd told him neither of the girls required such items of feminine hygiene yet, but she thought they should be on hand, "just in case." Dammit, bachelors weren't supposed to have to think about such details of child rearing. But despite that, he knew he didn't want any woman there in his private time. He had plenty of company from April to September, and the rest of the time he was there. But the fall was special. Usually until Christmas, he just wanted to paint, not be bothered by anyone, which was why he'd shot down Mel's original idea of hiring some young woman to help him with the kids. But neither did he want the girls' great-aunt up there with her fussy, old-maid ways, complaining about dirty socks and unwashed dishes and him being late for meals.

"No," he had said. "I don't want her here. The girls and I will get along just fine on our own. No, that's it, Mel," he added when she opened her mouth. "Really, it's best this way."

"Damn!" he said aloud now. "I should have known. I never should have trusted her. Those letters the girls kept writing. Melody put them up to it. And B.J. Is she in on it, too?"

"What's that, boss?" Fred asked, setting a pair of saddlebags on the kitchen table and balancing a small duffel bag on a chair. Cal reached out and took the helmet dangling from its strap over Fred's arm.

"Nothing. Never mind." He slammed the helmet onto the table and shot to his feet, fury burning through his very soul. Grabbing up *her* belongings, he stomped down the hall toward where he heard feminine laughter rising. With a peremptory knock on the door he swung it open. The three of them were lying across the bed, eyes lifted expectantly, two pair of brown, laughing, one pair of blue, startled.

"I have work to do," he said brusquely, dumping her things onto the dresser. "I'll be in the blind at the north end of the lake if there's an emergency, such as someone fainting or something equally dramatic. I'll probably spend the night there. Send Fred if I'm needed."

He wheeled around and left, leaving the bedroom door open, but his slamming of the back door reverberated through the house.

B.J. lay on the bed, stunned, gazing at the open doorway, her mind's eye seeing only the hard, angry face of the man who had just left. How could those gorgeous brown eyes change so quickly from glowing interest to glittering dislike?

And then it hit her. He'd remembered her—remembered ugly Janie. He was seeing the real Barbara Jane Gray, and hated himself for having been attracted to her . . . even in her present form. She felt sick. Her head hurt. Her chest ached. Dammit, it just wasn't fair! Why did some men go gaga over her, and Cal Mixall simply gag?

"Boy, what a grouch!" Laura said into the stunned silence Cal had left. "What's the matter with him?"

"I don't know," B.J. lied as she swallowed hard and slid off the bed. She went to the window and saw Cal step into a canoe and paddle across the lake. With each dip of his paddle it looked as if he were stabbing the water. That was one angry man, all right.

Well, she was angry, too, she realized, reveling in the feeling. It negated the hurt. And she was angry with better reason. What right did he have to react like that? She had every right to improve herself. He'd been disdainful of the way she'd been before, so why couldn't he congratulate her on the changes she worked so long and so hard to achieve? Oh, who cared what he thought, anyway? Not her!

She turned from the window to begin unpacking, and out of the corner of her eye, she saw the painting of the swan. She sighed, her anger fading as swiftly as it had risen. Even though she didn't want to, she understood his reaction. She'd even predicted it: the man was an artist, and one with a special insight. He revered reality, truth, and depicted it in painstaking detail. She represented out-and-out deception on every level, from her svelte figure to her golden hair to her blue eyes and her dimples. She was a fake and he'd spotted it. Of course he despised her.

As she unpacked B.J. listened to a long litany of complaints from the girls, a rehash of their letters, and finally, wearying of listening to their grumbles, she laughed and said, "Oh, knock it off, you two. Since when have you needed an adult to entertain you? And if your uncle says he's tired of 'whining and dining,' then my sympathy is with him. I'm sure his cooking isn't all that bad."

"It is so," Laura said huffily. "You adults always stick together. Mom and Dad do it, too, and it isn't fair."

"Life isn't, hon," B.J. said cheerfully, leaning back against the dresser to face the pair sitting on her bed. "But you still haven't told me anything that explains why you exaggerated so drastically in your letters in order to get me up here. What do you expect me to do? I can't just march into my host's kitchen and start cooking, you know."

"Mom does!"

"That's different."

"Anyway, we kind of hoped maybe Uncle Cal wouldn't work so hard if you were here," Kara said. "Laura said that maybe he'd fall for you and then he'd want to entertain—ouch!" She rubbed her pinched arm. "Laura, you did say that!"

"Oh, brother," B.J. said slowly, narrowing her gaze at her elder niece. "Does this mean what I think it means?"

"Well, she was right, wasn't she?" Laura said. "He does like you. He kissed you, B.J."

B.J.'s head spun as she sought an adequate explanation. "That . . . that was just an unfortunate impulse. He shouldn't have done it and I'm sure he regretted it as much as— *Who* was right?" She moaned. "Oh, don't bother telling me. Your mother! The plan was to get me up here with you from the very first. Lord, if I didn't know better, I'd suspect her of setting the school on fire!"

"But, B.J., if—"

B.J. straightened, her fists clenched at her sides. "But nothing, if nothing! I told her I wasn't interested in her precious brother-in-law! I told her I didn't even want to breathe the same air as he does! I told her to keep her nose out of my—" She broke off, drawing in a deep, steadying breath and slowly unclenching her fists. It was futile to tell Melody anything once the woman had made up her mind. And there was no point in ranting at a pair of innocent kids . . . though when it came to Laura, she wasn't terribly convinced of the degree of innocence.

"Tell me," she said conversationally, leaning back against the dresser again. "How did this all come about, anyway, your mother deciding that I should be here with you guys—and your uncle?" She added the last words venomously.

Laura explained, finishing by saying, "She asked me what I thought and I told her I thought it was a great idea. And I do, B.J. So does Kara. We'd love it if you and Uncle Cal fell in love and got married and we could be bridesmaids and aunts and baby-sitters, and well, it was Mom's idea, after all!"

"And it was a lousy idea," said her aunt, coming upright again and crossing her arms as she glared down at them. "Nobody has the right to play games with other people's lives. Now, you guys get this straight and you keep it straight: I do not like your uncle Cal. I do not want to marry him and live in the bushes. He does not like me. He does not want to

marry me and live in the city. I may well marry
someone someday, and if I do, I promise I'll ask you
both to be bridesmaids. If I ever have children, they
can call you 'aunt' and you can baby-sit. But I assure you, if I do any of those things, it will not be
with your uncle Calvin Mixall. Is that entirely clear?"

"Yes, ma'am."

"All right. We'll drop the subject." She unzipped
the jacket from the pants of her leather suit and
tugged it on. "Now, how'd you girls like to show me
around this wilderness your uncle loves so well?"

"B.J.?" said Kara in a small voice.

"Yes, honey?" B.J. took her hand and turned to
walk out of the room.

"How come you don't like Uncle Cal?"

B.J. paused, considered telling the truth, then
said gently, "Kara, that's really none of your business."

None of them saw the door in the other corridor
close softly, so none of them was aware that their
conversation had not been entirely private.

Cal stood leaning against the door to his studio.
He'd forgotten to pack the most basic essentials—
fresh pencils and enough paper—so he'd returned.
Lord, but he wished he hadn't. She didn't like him?
Dammit, why didn't she like him? She didn't even
know him! How could she have formed an opinion
so quickly?

But hadn't he formed an opinion just as quickly?
he asked himself. Of course he had. He had sat
there in the kitchen and remembered Melody's mach-
inations and assumed that B.J. had been part of
them. But now, having eavesdropped without com-
punction, he had enormous doubts. If she were part
of Mel's plot, why would she take such pains to tell
the girls otherwise?

No matter how much he hated to, he had to face

the facts. B.J. Gray was telling the simple truth when she told the kids she didn't like him, but in spite of that, she had tried to make them see his side of things, too. She was fair, then, as well as lovely. And forthright. And completely without guile. And he had misjudged her badly.

He sighed again and let himself out of the house, walked quietly back to the dock, and slipped into his canoe. This time he paddled slowly. She was something, that B.J. Gray. B for Barbara. That much seemed obvious. J for what? He thought about it. He considered and discounted Janet or Jean or Judith. No, it would be something exotic. Jasmine? Jonquil? Juniper? He would ask her. He frowned. If that were possible. Again, he heard her voice. *I do not like your uncle Cal.*

Dammit, he liked her, and somehow, he was going to make her like him.

It wasn't going to be easy, he realized, several hours later as he entered a kitchen full of the scent of good cooking. B.J. was stirring something in a big pot on the stove, and the aroma made his mouth water. That, for some reason he couldn't comprehend, made him furious all over again.

What right did she have to come roaring into his life like a small but elemental storm and turn him inside out? He should have stayed in the blind! He should go back and spend the next three or four days in the blind. How about six months? Or the rest of his life? It would be safer, for sure.

"What do you think you're doing?" he asked crossly, only half-ashamed of his irritable tone. It hid his deeper feelings, feelings he didn't want to acknowledge, but feelings that were growing stronger and stronger by the moment. The woman had been here a matter of hours. What kind of shape would he be in by Monday morning?

"Cooking stew," B.J. responded evenly, trying not

to sound as wary as she felt. Dammit, did he still think she had fainted to get his attention? Did he think she was crazy, or what? Now that he'd remembered fat, ugly Janie and knew her for what she really was, he must know better!

"I hope you don't mind," she went on evenly. "I found the meat in the deep freeze and used vegetables from the garden."

Her cool voice, the reserve in her blue eyes, defused his anger, and Cal found it impossible to speak for a minute. And he had to admit to himself that he didn't mind her cooking. Just the opposite. For some weird reason he loved the idea of her being in his kitchen. It was the first time in his life he had loved the idea of any woman there. Other than his sister-in-law and the camp cook in the summer. When it was one of them, he never gave it any thought. He shouldn't be giving it so much thought now, but he was—that, and several other things he shouldn't be giving any thought to. He had never chased after a woman in his life. If he'd felt that one didn't like him . . . He frowned. Had that ever happened? No, he guessed it hadn't. But still, if one had, he wouldn't have hung around her just for a chance to look at her, would he? Of course not. But with B.J. Gray, he had no choice. They had a mutual concern. Because of that, he had to hang around. Didn't he?

"Where are the girls?" he asked, to make conversation, to make her look at him.

"Doing their lessons."

Couldn't she even spare him one tiny smile? Couldn't she stop looking at him as if he were a worm and she might be considering putting him on a hook to feed to the sharks?

"You could be helping them with that," he said testily. "You don't have to cook for me. I can cook for myself. I've been doing it for years. I'd planned . . . something else for dinner." What, he hadn't the faintest idea, but now, suddenly, he wanted her out of his kitchen. He wanted her out from under his skin, before she took up permanent residence in either place.

With his full cooperation.

She flashed those dimples at him and he nearly fell down. Why did she have to be so beautiful, so dangerous to his peace of mind?

"Oh, this isn't for you," she said. "It's for the girls and me. We weren't expecting you. I'll be out of your way in a few minutes. It's nearly done now. I'm just waiting for the gravy to thicken."

Hunger assailed him again but he ignored it. He couldn't, however, ignore the hurt. Not for him? She wasn't even going to offer him any now that he was here? Hadn't she ever heard that the way to a man's heart was through his stomach?

He went into his room down the opposite wing from the girls' and her rooms, and slammed the door. Even through it, he could smell her cooking. Even in his shower he could smell it. Damn, damn, damn! It wasn't until his shower ran cold that he remembered she wouldn't be interested in the way to his heart. She didn't even like him.

Lord, how that rankled.

Three

When Cal came out of his bedroom, B.J. and the two kids were sitting at the table happily chatting and laughing, plates nearly empty, but a good half of the stew remained in the serving bowl on the table. He stood talking awkwardly to the girls for a few minutes, waiting for B.J. to invite him to share their meal. When she didn't, he slammed a frying pan onto the stove, chopped some onion into it, added a few strips of bacon, let that all cook for a while, then dumped a can of baked beans in on top.

To hell with her and her cooking. His was just fine. Maybe it didn't smell as great, but it smelled okay. Frying onion and bacon always did, but it didn't mask the spicy smell of that thick, rich stew the others were eating.

He had just sat down opposite B.J. with his plate of bacon and beans, when she finished her meal, asked the girls if they wanted more, was refused, and excused herself. She stood up and took the bowl of stew from the table. "There," she said, snapping plastic wrap over the top of it and setting it in the refrigerator. "That will do for lunch tomorrow, girls. Ready for your turnovers now?"

Turnovers?

He didn't look. He wouldn't look. He refused to look at the pan she took from the oven, but how was he supposed to avoid it when she set it down not six inches from his plate? He felt weak. Four turnovers. Four beautiful, golden, flaky-crusted turnovers smelling of apples and nutmeg and cinnamon. Quickly, he began to shovel in his beans.

"Here, Laura," B.J. said, setting one of the turnovers on a small plate. She covered it with a napkin and handed it to her niece. "Why don't you take that over to Fred while it's still warm? I'm sure he'll appreciate it, and he was so good about repairing that greenhouse."

Feeling betrayed, Cal watched as the extra apple turnover went swiftly out the door. Hell! Who paid Fred's wages? Who had paid for the glass? Who deserved that turnover more? Who owned the damned apples? Not Fred!

They didn't lick their plates, but they did rinse them off and set them in the dishwasher, and then B.J. said graciously, "Are you finished, Cal? I'll put your plate in if you are."

He shoved it toward her and sat glowering at the table. He knew he was sulking, just as he had accused the girls of sulking, knew he must look as ridiculous to the others as the kids did to him when they pouted. He glanced up under his dark brows. Others? Make that other. No kids. Just one woman. Just B.J. Just B.J. and her blue eyes and her pink sweater and her skintight black pants and her golden, shimmery hair—and him.

He got to his feet, not at all amused to find that his knees were shaking. She was deftly filling the coffee maker as if she had spent ten years in his kitchen, using his appliances, stepping around him when he got in the way, the same as Melody did with Curtis. She glanced up at him and smiled and suddenly he wanted her so badly he could have screamed. If she hated his guts, why did she smile at him? He wanted to grab her. He remembered how she had felt in his arms while she was wearing thick leather over her clothes. He wondered how she'd feel with just clothes on. Or with no clothes.

He wanted to see how she'd fit in the kitchen of his house in West Vancouver. No, not the kitchen. He had someone there already. So how about in the living room? Oh, hell, let's face it, he wanted to see her in the bedroom in the worst way. He wanted . . . lots of things.

"Why don't you like me?" he asked abruptly. Even to his own ears, he sounded like a seven-year-old who was being chased out of the playground by the other kids. Oh, Lord, what was the matter with him, letting her know he had snooped on a private conversation? *Letting her know that it mattered?*

B.J. met his gaze, startled and unhappy, and bit her lip. "I'm sorry," she said. "I didn't mean for you to hear that."

It appalled her that he had. She hated to hurt other people; she knew too well how it felt. Dammit, how had he heard her? She could only assume he'd come back to the house more quietly than he'd slammed out of it. Obviously, he'd been eavesdropping, and though eavesdroppers were traditionally not supposed to hear any good about themselves— take her, for instance—she was deeply ashamed and sorry that she'd hurt him. Maybe it was poetic justice, but she was so ashamed of herself she wanted to crawl away and hide. Not only had she bellowed to the kids that she didn't like the man, failing to offer him some of that stew had been nothing short of churlish. She would have, *had* planned on telling him there was some left for him, but when he'd come in with such an attitude toward her, it had got her Irish up and . . .

She swallowed hard and looked down at the counter, not wanting to go on meeting the distress in his eyes, and not wanting him to see what was in hers. "Please, forgive me for being so rude. I didn't mean to hurt your feelings."

"You . . . didn't," he lied, but he noticed that she didn't deny disliking him and that hurt his pride all over again. "I just wondered . . . why?"

She shrugged helplessly and turned from him.

"Dammit," he said roughly, putting his hands on that soft, pink sweater, feeling the woman right through it as he urged her to face him. At once, she lifted troubled eyes to his. All the anger left him.

"Ah, B.J. . . ." He wanted to tell her it was all right, that she didn't have to feel bad about not liking him, that he could live with it—but he couldn't. He couldn't tell her that, and he couldn't live with it.

"You told Kara it was none of her business," he said. "That may have been true. But when somebody takes a dislike to me, I think it really is my business."

"Yes," she agreed, "I suppose it is, but it's not something I can explain. I don't see why it matters; I know you don't like me either. And you never wanted me here."

She smiled again, but not very happily, and stepped neatly from his hands. "I promise I won't stay long." Her chin tilted up an inch or two and she added, "Nor did I faint to get your attention."

For some reason her honesty irked him. Why couldn't she pretend he'd never been sarcastic and suggested, however obliquely, that she might have purposefully fainted? Or at least pretend that she hadn't understood him? It had only been his anger and—all right—his fear talking, but now that she'd reminded him, he knew it had made him sound arrogant and conceited and . . . unlikable. But, dammit, if she could be truthful, then so could he.

"You didn't have to faint to get my attention. You already had it. And you're right. I didn't want you here. I mean, I don't. But if it's better for the kids, now that you're here, maybe you should stay."

Oh, Lord, had he really said that? Yes, he had, and the worst part was that he meant it. Far from wanting her to go so that he could get his cavorting libido back to normal, he wanted her there, stirring him up, because he liked the kind of stirring she did.

She looked startled, almost scared, and whirled away. "No," she said, scrubbing vigorously at the stove top. She shook her head, and little lights danced from her hair like golden sparkles. "The girls will adapt, and like I said earlier, I'm house-sitting for a friend who hates to leave his place unattended. Burglaries, you know. Besides, he has a cockatoo."

"Burglaries?" Cal said sharply. He couldn't have cared less about some other guy's cockatoo. "And just what the hell would you do if somebody did break in?" The picture that formed in his mind was unpleasant, to say the least.

"Call the police, of course," she replied calmly as she rinsed the cloth. She dried her hands, then reached up into a cupboard to get down two coffee mugs. Her sweater stretched taut over her breasts, and he felt sweat break out on the back of his neck. His chest was so tight he could barely speak.

"Call the police, sure, and in the meantime the guy comes busting through the door and murders you."

"Oh, come on. The house is in Vancouver, not Los Angeles."

"Nobody gets murdered in Vancouver?"

"I'm not saying that. But the chances of my being

murdered by a burglar in Vancouver are considerably less, I think."

"The chances of your being murdered here at Kinikinik Lake are even less than that," he retorted, snatching one of the mugs from her and filling it with coffee. Stubborn woman! He was offering her safety, for Pete's sake. Security. And she continued to say no.

Fuming, he stalked out, only to return a few seconds later. He set his cup onto the table and stood right before her.

"You know what, B.J. Gray?" he asked belligerently.

"I might, after all, get murdered at Kinikinik Lake?" she asked, and suddenly he got the impression she was laughing at him.

He let out a long breath, watching it ruffle her bangs. If she could laugh at him, then so could he. He had to laugh. He had been behaving like an arrogant jerk.

"No," he said, amazed at the softness of his tone. "I just want to tell you that you have the prettiest eyes I have ever seen in my entire life. And your hair . . . it shimmers."

"Oh." It was all she could manage, due to the breathless excitement engendered by the look in his dark, laughing eyes. Elated, she realized one important thing: he hadn't recognized her after all. The relief made her dizzy, and she would have swayed but for the support of the chair back she gripped with one hand.

"Yes," he said, as if she had questioned him. Then he lifted a hand and stroked her cheek. "And the most beautiful skin." His fingers trailed down over her jaw as heat curled and twisted inside her. When he touched her throat, she tried to move, and could not. "And I don't regret for one minute having kissed you."

"Cal—" she began, on the verge of telling him who

she was, telling him things that would remind him of that time before, but he cut her off by placing two fingers over her mouth.

"And I plan to do it again very, very soon."

Involuntarily, she licked her lips, her tongue making brief contact with his fingers. She saw desire flare in his eyes, but he pivoted and headed out the door.

B.J. watched him stalk off toward his lair and stifled a sigh. The sooner she got out of there, the better, she decided, determined not to let the girls' pleadings change her mind. She'd stay until Monday morning, and then she'd be gone. Calvin Mixall was too potent a danger for her even to consider spending any more time here than was necessary.

She spent the rest of the evening ignoring the fact that he was just down the hall in his studio, working as, the girls said, he did every evening. Although he'd come out briefly to help tuck the girls in—when she went to bed he was still working. She lay there in the darkness wondering at the deep restlessness within her soul. It was like . . . hunger, and hunger was something she hadn't experienced for a long time, but it was a different kind of hunger.

She knew what it was. She wasn't a fool, and didn't try to kid herself. She was responding to Calvin Mixall as a woman responds to a man, but she couldn't give in to it, couldn't let it govern her actions. This time she would be in control.

She bit her lip, knowing her control might not hold if he touched her again. He appealed to her too strongly. He had appealed to her just as strongly once before, she reminded herself. She rolled onto her stomach as she heard his footsteps—or imagined them—in the other wing of the lodge.

She had seen pictures of him before she met him for the first time, and had thought he was the most handsome man she had ever seen. But when he arrived with his parents to spend the weekend for Curt and Melody's wedding, she had discovered that Cal in the flesh far outshone his photographs. She'd been captivated by his looks. His personality, though, had been something else again.

He had been remote, gloomy, and his funereal attitude had nearly driven her sister Phyllis wild. As the mother of the bride, Phyllis didn't have time to entertain the groom's sullen younger brother. "For heaven's sake," she had said to B.J. after three hours of watching Cal sit in morose silence, "do something with him. Show him around the city. Give him the grand tour."

Her? she had thought. Phyllis wanted her to do that? She had been terrified, certain he'd refuse, but he'd shrugged and gone along with her. From that moment on, she had seen nothing but his beautiful face, his long, lean, graceful body, and his smile. Oh, that smile! It had come rarely at first, but when it did, it had dazzled her. Then, as they became friends—or so she had thought—it had flashed into his eyes often, but thrilling her no less each time.

She had never thought herself capable of entertaining a man . . . until that weekend. But with him to bring her out of herself, to get her talking, she had felt if not scintillating, pretty, then, at least, almost . . . acceptable.

And then, a couple of days later, the wedding, the reception . . . and reality.

With a groan, B.J. turned onto her side, drawing her knees up close to her chest. She knew she would not tell him the truth about herself unless he asked her. Because if she did, and his reaction turned out to be exactly what she had thought it had been today, she wouldn't be able to bear it.

She sat up, frowning. So why had he been angry today? She shook her head, unable to come up with a satisfactory answer. Unless it was simply because he knew he was attracted to her, just as an ordinary woman, and didn't want to be. Maybe, strange as it might seem, he was just as afraid of the powerful magnetism between them as she was. And if that were the case . . .

Please, she prayed, *don't ever let him remember me as I used to be!*

Cal was gone when B.J. and the girls got up on Friday morning, and he spent the entire day away. When he returned late in the evening, though, after the girls had gone to bed, he didn't go to his studio. He joined her in the lounge where she was watching an old John Wayne movie.

"Mind if I watch with you?" he asked, hovering a few feet away.

"Of course not." What could she say? This was his house. Besides, some adult company would be nice, she told herself, not admitting that she had been waiting all day to see him—even if she was half-afraid.

"Would you like a glass of wine?" he asked. "Or something else? We have a well-stocked bar here, even though my sister-in-law calls the place Spartan."

"Wine would be nice," she said, and he smiled, causing something inside her to turn over. She watched as he walked to the far side of the room and lifted two glasses down from a cupboard behind a short bar. Moving to the end of the bar, he crouched and opened a small refrigerator, selecting a tall, green bottle. As he stood, his muscular thighs tautened the faded material of his jeans. He moved with a smooth, feline grace. Once, she had likened him to a sleek black panther, and nothing had changed, even though he was twelve years older. There was a leashed power about him that she found devastatingly seductive.

She should have said no and left as soon as he

offered her a drink. She'd be safer locked in her room, yet she'd forgotten about the dangerous, insidious feelings his smile could evoke. Or if she hadn't exactly forgotten, she'd ignored the danger with an uncustomary boldness. It wasn't safe to stay there with him, but it was too late, she told herself, because he was back, passing her a tall stemmed glass filled with pale golden liquid. If she ran now, he'd know what a coward she was.

Sitting at the opposite end of the sofa, he put his feet up on an ottoman and leaned back, one arm stretched along the couch back. Raising his glass, he said, "Cheers. Did you and the girls find enough to keep you busy today?"

"Yes, thanks."

"What did you do?"

"Oh, this and that."

"You're not being very communicative."

"I'm sorry. The girls showed me around. We hiked a bit, but they said we couldn't go too far afield because the grizzlies are fattening up for winter. This is a beautiful place."

Leaning back, he drank some wine, and then said softly, "B.J., I think we got off to a bad start yesterday. I was rude to you, and I apologize. I certainly haven't acted very likable. But I'd like a chance to change your mind about me. Could we try to be friends?"

Her heart hammered painfully. "I . . . don't see any reason why not," she said, so untruthfully, she wondered why her nose didn't grow. "I apologize, too, because I've been less than . . . well, friendly." Her laugh was soft and apologetic. "A friendly woman wouldn't have given away that extra turnover when there was someone looking at it the way you were."

He smiled, making her heart race. "I forgive you. You were—provoked. Now, tell me about B.J. Gray," he said. "To begin with, what does the J stand for? I decided it had to be something exotic."

Such a simple question, she thought, and one she should answer without hesitation. But her tongue seemed frozen to the roof of her mouth. If he knew, would he remember being introduced to Janie?

"Don't disappoint me, okay?"

She drew in a deep breath and tried to treat his question as she knew Melody would have. "I wouldn't dream of it! Who am I to spoil a man's fantasies? You go right on thinking I have an exotic middle name. When you come up with one I like, maybe I'll adopt it." She sipped her wine, and then asked, "What brought you to such an unlikely location? I mean, it's a bit off the beaten track for—" She broke off, looking down into her wine.

"For what?" He looked genuinely interested.

"For an artist of your caliber, who clearly needs an active social life among the right people in order to promote his work."

"Well." He blinked. "You do think you have me pegged, don't you?"

B.J. knew she was flushing. "No, of course not. I don't know you, so how could I have you pegged? But Melody sometimes mentions you." Smiling faintly, she added, "So do the papers."

He looked grim for a moment. "Don't believe everything you read, B.J."

"I . . . no. I try not to. How did you come here then? What attracted you to a place like this?"

He smiled slowly. "Swans." His face changed, taking on an eager glow. "Trumpeter swans. I heard that they wintered here and made arrangements to spend a few weeks so I could study and paint them. Then, when the California church group who owned Kinikinik put the place on the market, I snapped it up."

"Because of the swans?" She didn't try to hide her surprise and curiosity.

His smile deepened and his eyes shone. "That's right."

She stayed quiet, letting him think whatever thoughts made him so happy. After a few moments he seemed to recall her presence and flicked his gaze over her. "I use the place as a tax shelter, too, of course. The operating expenses cut my taxable income considerably. It's more than just self-indulgence."

She wondered at his defensiveness and smiled. "That's okay. You don't have to justify yourself to me." Heavens no, she thought. What she had done with part of her inheritance had been pure self-indulgence, but so necessary and so worthwhile in the end that she could never regret having spent the thousands she had. Nor did she regret the time and the effort, the months of dieting to reach her present weight of one hundred and ten.

"I wasn't trying to justify myself," he said gruffly. "Or if I was, it was only through force of habit." He touched her cheek with the back of one hand, a brief caress, but one that tingled right through her. "I thought I saw disapproval in those pretty blue eyes. Maybe because I'm so used to getting it from my parents."

"They don't like Kinikinik Lake?"

"They don't like much I do."

From Curtis, B.J. knew that was true. The elder Mixalls disapproved of both of their sons. An artist and an art dealer were not what they had thought they were raising. The very macho owner of one of the country's largest trucking firms had expected, if not truck drivers, then at least businessmen interested in running the company from its Toronto main office.

"My father considers buying an entire lake, even with an active fifteen-bedroom guest lodge thrown in, a bit excessive," Cal went on with a low laugh. "At least since my prime reason was to keep a flock of trumpeter swans company."

His chuckle was warm and she liked the sound of it. "But self-indulgence or not, I found I needed this place. Those magnificent birds were an inducement I couldn't resist. And as long as I own this lake, nobody is going to be using the lead shot that kills so many of them every year in other places."

He got up and reached down a hand for her. Automatically, she took it and he tugged her to her feet. He led her into the dining room, where a large oil painting hung beside a stone fireplace, showing a pair of white birds with graceful necks and long black beaks. They were of the same breed as the one in the painting in her bedroom. One stood splay-footed on a sheet of ice, head lifted toward the other as if in welcome. The second bird, its huge wings outspread, the light of a pale sun opalescing through the tips and edges, was coming in to land beside its mate. Somehow, Cal had captured the sense of their bonding. The one on the ice was happy the other was there, was bidding it welcome. If they had been humans, they'd have been running toward each other with arms outstretched.

"Look at them, B.J.," he said almost reverently. "Aren't they incredible?"

"They are beautiful," she said, supremely conscious of the warmth of his fingers around her hand. The birds impressed her, but not as much as the man who had captured their inner beauty. "How big are they? And why are they called trumpeters?"

"They're the largest North American bird," he told her, his gaze still on the painting, "with a wingspan greater even than the bald eagle, although eagles do prey on their young, along with wolves and coyotes." He turned and looked down at her, his eyes agleam with pleasure. "I've been immersed in a love affair with them since I first saw them come winging in here out of a sky so blue it made my eyes ache, calling with voices that filled the entire valley. They were named trumpeters because of their call, but a thousand human trumpeters could never make the same kind of music that a hundred of those birds can. Oh, but they're something! You have to see them and hear them to know what I mean. They're so majestic, they do something to my soul."

Turning, still holding her hand, he led her back to the lounge. He seated her on the couch, then refilled their glasses before sitting down beside her. He gave her an account of the life history of the birds he loved, and as he talked, his fingers touched the back of her hair, toying with it idly as if he were unaware he was doing so. B.J. didn't dare move, and something fluttered inside her as she watched his animated face, heard the passion in his voice.

"They were once nearly extinct because of over-hunting. They were shot and skinned, and the skins shipped away to Europe."

"Skins? They were skinned like furbearing animals?"

"Yes. And for the same reason. Fashion, mostly. Women's muffs were stuffed with swansdown. They made powder puffs out of it, and the quills were used for pens. By the end of the nineteenth century, the swans were seriously endangered. In 1916 there were only an estimated one hundred of the birds left in the entire world."

"You said 'once' nearly extinct? Are they safe now?"

"Yes," he said with satisfaction. "And it's all thanks to one couple and their daughter. In the twenties and thirties, a couple named Edwards, up north of here, took an interest in the plight of the birds and started feeding them." He shook his head. "That man . . . he was some kind of a hero. You must have heard of him. Ralph Edwards of Lonesome Lake. Books have been written about him, and at least one movie made. Each year he carried hundreds of pounds of seed—on his back, because there were no roads—to feed those birds, and brought their numbers back. Now the swans range all over the province and down into Washington, maybe Oregon, and winter on many lakes and coastal inlets. When Edwards was no longer able to continue his work, his daughter, Trudy, took over. She learned to fly a plane partly so she could feed the swans."

"Do you feed them?"

"No. There's no need now. The flock is strong enough to let nature care for them, and there's plenty of food here. You saw how red their heads and necks were?" She nodded. "They feed underwater, and get stained by the silt at the bottom of the lake. That's also why they are dying in great numbers from lead shot. It sinks to the bottom and they scoop it up as they feed. But not here," he added. "Here, at least, they're safe."

"And you spend the winters here to make sure they stay that way?" She was amazed and touched by his love of the big birds. Was this the same man who for so long she'd believed to be insensitive?

"I don't spend the winters here," he said. "I come up for a few weeks to paint the swans, and just to visit them, but I must wait until the lake's frozen solid so I can use skis on the plane." He smiled and touched her hair again. "I'd like you to see them, B.J. Those swans are a sight to behold. Will you come? In the winter?" Almost as an afterthought, he added, "And the girls, of course."

B.J. smiled. "That would be nice," she said noncommittally. Of course she wouldn't be coming up there in the winter. Not even with the girls.

She wanted to move away from that soft, tantalizing touch on her hair. He had fixed her with a warm gaze, though, and she couldn't force her body to action. She was too deliciously conscious of his fingertips slipping lazily through her curls, brushing her nape lightly, sending tingles down her spine. Her nipples tightened and little flutters warmed her lower belly. She shivered, knowing she wanted him, wondering why she had never wanted anyone else in exactly this same way.

Was this what she had been waiting for for so many years? Was he the reason she had resisted the advances of other men? Because she had known, somewhere on some hidden level, that Cal Mixall was in the world, and when she looked good enough to please him, he would want her? She tried to breathe and felt her breath catch in her throat. She knew he heard it, because his fingers tightened in her hair and his face became very still as his gaze held hers.

"I think it's time," he said softly.

"For what?"

"For that kiss we've both been waiting for."

Four

"What? We aren't . . . I mean, I haven't been . . ."
B.J. stopped, drew in a deep breath, and tried again.
"No, it's not," she said, this time managing to proj-
ect a calm she didn't feel. Dammit, what was the
matter with her? It wasn't as though no man had
ever given her advance notice of his intentions before. But never had such notice sent her into such a
panic. It was, she knew, simply because it was Cal
Mixall sitting there touching her, gazing at her, his
intentions clear in his slumberous eyes. Quickly,
she moved away, getting to her feet and putting
distance between them.

"It's time to say good night instead," she said.

Rising, Cal took the empty glass from her fingers
and set it down. He touched the tip of her nose.
"You're running away."

Of course she was running away. She wasn't stupid. He was more than she could handle and she
knew it. "I'm tired."

He grinned. "Does that mean you won't be able to
run very fast?"

She lifted her brows. "I'm sure I won't have to,"

she said. "I doubt that you're the kind of man who ever forces his attentions on a woman."

He tapped her nose again and laughed. "How prim that sounds, Miss Gray. Are you prim? Have you said no?"

She hesitated. Was she prim? She'd never thought so before. But with him, maybe primness would be a saving grace. Aloud she said, "I don't think so. But as I said, I am tired. Good night." She moved quickly, but not quickly enough, because he captured her and held her still while he gazed into her eyes.

"You didn't answer my other question," he reminded her, quite unnecessarily. She knew perfectly well she hadn't. He repeated it very softly. "Have you said no to me, B.J.? Are you saying that?"

She tried to draw in a breath, but her throat was too tight. Her voice had no force as she said, "Cal . . . please." He nodded as if he understood that she didn't want to be asked, which was something she hadn't understood herself until that moment. Then he kissed her until her eyes closed, and she would have slumped except that he was holding her up. When he lifted his head and she opened her eyes, he was looking at her with a strangely speculative expression, and frowning slightly.

She stepped back from him. "Good night," she managed to say. She turned and headed out of the room.

"B.J."

His voice made her hesitate, and she glanced back at him. He hadn't moved.

"Are we going to be friends?" he asked.

Were they? "I don't know."

"But . . . we aren't enemies, are we?"

She drew in a deep breath and let it out slowly, silently. "No. No, Cal. We don't have to be enemies."

"Good." With three long strides, he was beside

her. His arms were around her and he was kissing her long and hard and deeply, his tongue sweeping aside any barrier she might have put up and tasting every crevice within the heat of her mouth. Lifting his head, he looked at her, again with that puzzled, considering expression. "Kiss me back, B.J.," he said in a soft, growly voice that rubbed over her nerves like silk velvet. "Like you did before."

"When I . . ." she started to say, but he didn't give her a chance to finish, only took her mouth once more in another devastating kiss. *Like you did before* . . . His words echoed in her whirling mind. What had he meant? What had she done before that pleased him? She had only tried to taste him. She flicked out the tip of her tongue and stroked it over his lower lip . . . and felt him shudder. His arms tightened around her and he groaned softly, licking her upper lip just as she'd done to his bottom one. It felt . . . incredible, and heat curled in little flickering flames all over her body. He did it again, and she trembled, clenching her fists in his hair.

"Oh, lady, but you do things to me," he breathed when he lifted his head. "Open your eyes. Look at me."

Her heart full of wonder, she obeyed. His eyes were jet black and bottomless, and his breath ragged. He lifted a hand and touched a spot on her throat. "There," he said. "There it is. That fascinates me, B.J."

Under the pressure of his fingertip, she could feel the wild pulse in her throat. It throbbed everywhere, not just where he touched. For a moment she could only stare at him, then she, too raised a hand and touched him. High in his temple, just at his hairline, a pulse hammered. Smiling, she stroked her fingers over it. "You have one, too."

With that, she slipped out of his hold and was

gone, and Cal stood for a long time, thinking, before he turned off the lights and retired.

Cal finished his breakfast and shoved his plate away. "That," he said, "was one of the most satisfying meals I've had in a long time. Thanks B.J. I'm grateful."

"You're welcome," she said. "I was cooking for myself and the girls, so a few extra hotcakes was no trouble at all." She smiled, and her dimples winked in and out. He wanted very badly to kiss them, and her lips. Her lips . . . He didn't think she'd kissed many men, as incredible as that seemed, but she sure was a quick study. To distract himself he stood to fill her coffee cup and his own, then sat down across from her, studying her again.

Under his scrutiny, she felt nervous . . . or maybe restless. At any rate, she wished he'd quit studying her so closely.

"Last night," he said, "you very neatly turned me aside when I asked you to tell me about yourself. Instead, we ended up talking about my work. This morning let's talk about yours."

She shrugged. "I'm a teacher. What's to talk about?"

"To start with, how long have you been teaching?"

"Eight years. Nearly nine, I guess."

"And in a boarding school. Is that why I've never met you? I mean, I've lived in British Columbia for two years, we have mutual family, so you'd have thought we'd have bumped into each other at least once or twice."

B.J. shifted uncomfortably, thinking of the fights she'd had with Melody so she wouldn't be "inadvertently" invited to Mel's at the same time as Cal. *No accidents*, she'd warned. *Even one, Melody, and I won't come back here again.*

"I suppose it's just the way our schedules have worked out," she said. "Your time up here covers the major part of the time—summer—when I'm not in school."

"You live at the school, don't you?"

"Yes. Odd, now that I think of it, but all of my teaching jobs have required me to live in. My first one was in an orphanage in Peru."

Cal's eyes widened. "Peru? Why?"

She shrugged. "Why not?" She wasn't about to tell him that she had tried to get a job nearer home. She'd had several interviews, none of which had panned out, and she had finally come to the conclusion that no school board was about to hire a twenty-one-year-old inexperienced teacher who could barely make it through the door of the classroom—not when there were so many others out there who were physically fit. "I speak excellent Spanish and they were looking for an English teacher. I qualified and they hired me." *Sight unseen,* she added silently. *And then the food had been so terrible she'd begun losing weight.* After the first six months, when she'd realized what was happening to her body, she had begun a tentative, timid exercise program to see if she could speed things up. Somehow, for some reason, that time, it had all worked.

"How long did you stay there?" he asked.

"Two years." She smiled, remembering the children she had come to love, remembering the joy and sorrow when one or another was finally taken in by a real family, and the agony on the rare occasions when the adoption didn't work out and the child was returned.

Watching her face, Cal reached across the table and touched her hand, curling his fingers over hers. "You loved it," he said, "but part of it made you sad?"

Narrowing her eyes at him, she said, "Artist!" as though it were an expletive.

He laughed. "I can't help it. You have a very expressive face. Why did you leave the orphanage? And where did you go after that?"

"Brazil." Why had she left the orphanage? Because she had lost nearly eighty pounds by then and one man, a trustee, who just happened to like generously plump women, and who also just happened to be married, wouldn't leave her alone. She, who had never had to deal with sexual harassment before, had been ill equipped to handle it, and the nuns in charge of the orphanage had pooh-poohed her complaints. Señor Mendoza was a good man, a family man, and she was allowing ordinary friendliness to frighten her.

"Brazil was wonderful," she said. "I taught the eight children of one family—the da Silvas—and about a dozen children of people who worked for them on their estate."

"I can see you enjoyed it," he said. "What was best about it?"

"Horses!" Her smile softened. "They were—are—a wonderful family. They breed horses, and since all the children rode, and I lived as a member of the family, I had to learn as well. It was fantastic." But only after she'd managed to dump another sixty pounds. Then the riding had been just the right exercise to help her shed the rest of her fat.

"Do you ride?" she asked.

Cal shook his head. "Neither motorcycles nor horses, though I'd like to try a bike sometime. I took horseback lessons as a child, but it was never one of my favorite pastimes. Around and around and around a track was about as boring as it could get."

"I'm sure it was. That wasn't the way I learned to ride." She laughed, eyes alight as she remembered.

"The da Silvas' head groom taught me, and after a day of leading me around and around as you put it, he decreed me ready to ride. We took off across the prairie at a nice easy lope that wiped me out in only twenty minutes. For the next two days I could barely crawl out of bed, but crawl I did, right back onto my horse. Within a month I was flying like the wind and it was the first time in my life I had felt real freedom of movement and—" She broke off, aware that she was saying too much. Drat the man! How easily he could make her forget herself. How easy it was to talk to him. But she should have remembered that, shouldn't she?

The only other man she had ever felt as relaxed with had been Antonio. . . .

Cal squeezed her hand. "You were saying?"

She pulled her hand out from under his and got to her feet, beginning to load the dishwasher. "It was . . . a good time in my life, and I'd still be with them, I suppose, only Dom Carlos was named Ambassador to Australia. It seemed he knew there was that possibility and that was why I was hired to teach his children English."

"Couldn't you have gone with them?"

She leaned her elbows back behind her on the counter and stared down at the floor. "They asked me to, but another family on a nearby estate wanted me to teach their children. And by that time, my Portuguese was almost as good as my Spanish and I wanted to keep it going, so I stayed." And there was Antonio, son of another neighbor, and she had been half in love with him. . . .

Cal stood and tilted her chin up with one hand. "And?"

Dammit, she wished he'd quit reading her face. "And what?"

"There's more," he said.

"Of course, isn't there always?" She pulled free of him. "But I should go out and see what the girls are up to."

At that moment Laura and Kara rushed in, all rosy-cheeked and sweet smelling like the crisp, mountain air. "When are you coming out, B.J.?" Kara asked.

"In a minute. I'll just start the dishwasher."

"What are you going to do today?" Cal asked them.

"I don't know." Laura looked at her aunt. "B.J.? What are we going to do?"

The girls didn't, Cal noticed, look sad or bored or lonely now, and they hadn't sulked since B.J. had come. They both had an eager shine about their faces, as if they knew the day was going to be full and busy and exciting.

Desperately, he wanted to join in whatever they were going to do—as long as they were going to do it with his unexpected house guest.

"Lots of things," B.J. said, "but first I want to check out my bike and free up those brakes. I should have done it yesterday."

"I checked your bike," Cal said, watching her slide her arms into the sleeves of her jacket. "It's a bit scratched, but not damaged. I fixed the brakes and looked it over completely to make sure it was safe for you to ride."

"Thank you." He could see she was surprised. "It was . . . nice of you to look at it for me."

"I'm a nice person," he said without smiling.

To his chagrin, she didn't comment on that. She smiled slightly, not enough to activate her dimples, but certainly enough to turn his insides over at an alarming rate. "I could have checked it out myself, you know. I try to maintain it myself. It only makes sense when I ride so much off the beaten track."

"I thought you were a city woman, preferring paved

roads to the . . . bushes." Her disliking the wilderness bothered him, but he didn't know why. It wasn't as though he wanted her to want to live there, for Pete's sake. She didn't have to find his life-style compatible. He didn't live there year round himself.

"I am a city person," she agreed. "But I still like the country. As an escape."

"Escape from what?"

She jammed her slender hands into the pockets of her jacket and shrugged. "From . . . I don't know. Just from routine, I guess."

"Routine. Yes." He wondered what her routine consisted of. He wondered, too, why she had clammed up a few minutes ago and looked relieved when the girls came in. What was there about her life that she didn't want him to know? "And I'd better get to mine," he added. "Enjoy your morning, girls, and don't forget to do your lessons sometime today."

He laughed and apologized, making a swift escape under a flurry of cries about it's being Saturday, Uncle Cal! And they didn't have to do lessons on weekends, did they?

Behind him, he heard B.J. assuring them that he'd simply forgotten the day of the week. He wasn't being an ogre.

Yes, he thought, firmly placing himself in front of his easel, he'd forgotten the day of the week, all right. He was lucky he could remember his own name.

Her bike, as Cal had said, had suffered no damage beyond a few scrapes to its already battered coat of paint. B.J. took it for a short test run, then spent an hour giving the girls rides in turn, trying to keep her mind off the man working in a room not three hundred feet away.

Thoughts of him, though, constantly intruded, until she thought she would go crazy. What was his studio like? How did he achieve that amazing realism he was famous for? Some critics had said that you could tell an animal painted by Calvin Mixall because you could see it breathing, hear it snarling, watch its hairs lifting in the wind. The night before, when he'd been talking about the swans, she could see how much he loved them. He must feel that way about all wildlife, she mused, for his paintings to be so successful. Did that mean he didn't have the same love for his own kind? He never painted people, did he?

"Teach me to ride all by myself," Laura begged.

"Why not?" she said, thinking that maybe having something to concentrate on would keep her mind in a track she could deal with. "Your legs are long enough."

"Why *not*?" Cal asked behind them, making B.J. and the girls whirl around. "Because it's a crazy idea, is why not!"

He looked outraged, standing there with his hands on his lean hips, his legs long in his jeans, his shoulders broad within a powder blue cotton shirt. Dammit, he was too appealing, B.J. thought, with his black eyes alive and sparkling as he looked at her as if she had just offered to teach Laura to skydive with a bedsheet for a parachute.

"You aren't old enough, Laura," he said, "even though you might be tall enough, and the trails around here are rough going for a beginner." His tone, B.J. noticed, had softened considerably. She liked that about him. Even though he was refusing his niece something she wanted, he was prepared to be reasonable about it, and explain to her why he had to do it.

"But, Uncle Cal . . ."

"I'm sorry. Your parents didn't say anything at all about your being allowed to ride a motorcycle. And as your guardian, I feel compelled to say no, so let's just forget the idea, okay?"

Laura glared at him rebelliously, then wailed, "But B.J.'s our guardian, too, and she should have just as much say in the matter and she said she'd teach me!" Her eyes filled with tears and her face crumpled.

"And I said she's not." Cal was beginning to look more than just a little disconcerted.

"And I happen to agree with your uncle," B.J. said quickly, hugging Laura in apology. "While you're here at his place, he makes the rules, as is only right. If you were with me, then I'd make them. When I said I'd teach you, I wasn't thinking clearly. The trails here *are* too rough for a beginner, to say nothing of too steep. Look what happened to me, and I've been riding for years and years! I'd hate to have to call your parents and confess that I'd done something stupid and let you get injured."

Cal gaped at her. He'd seen the flare of anger in her eyes when he first spoke. He'd cut off what he expected to be a heated argument, and to have her agree with him was so unexpected, he didn't know how to handle it. So what else was new? Since her arrival, the woman had made a habit of throwing him off balance. But still, what she'd done required some kind of acknowledgment on his part. Other than his kissing her feet. He blinked, thinking about that. He'd start there and—

"I . . . well, thank you, Miss Gray."

She grinned at the blank astonishment on his face. "Thank you, Mr. Mixall. See? I'm a fairly nice person myself, and I was about to make a mistake. I'm glad you came along in time to stop me. So, ladies, what should we do now? Any more suggestions for some fun and excitement at Kinikinik Lake?"

"How about a canoe trip?" Cal asked, then frowned at his own words. What he should do was go back into his studio and work. If he meant to have enough pieces ready for that show in December, he couldn't afford to waste time now. He'd been telling the girls that ever since they came. About to recant his invitation, he opened his mouth and said, "To the end of the lake and back."

"You're very good," Cal said half an hour later as he looked across ten feet of rippled water, watching the steady, quiet rhythm with which B.J. propelled the canoe she and Kara were in. He liked to see her body in motion. Her arms, covered only by the sleeves of her blue baseball jersey, were slender but sinuously strong, and even the yellow floater vest couldn't hide the shape of her breasts from him. As always, he was painfully aware of her.

"Thank you," she said. "I like canoeing. One summer I did the whole Bowron Lake circuit with a friend."

He stared ahead for some time, thinking about the Bowron Lake circuit, the quiet little bays where camp could be set up in seclusion, where it was so private that swimmers needed no suits, where it was so peaceful that couples could— He cut his thoughts off at that point. Dammit, it was none of his business!

Moments later he heard himself say tautly, "I know a few people who've done that circuit. What's your friend's name?"

"Terry Milligan."

Oh, thanks a bunch! he said silently, digging his paddle in harder and shooting his canoe ahead of hers. That really told him what he wanted to know.

B.J. saw Cal's muscles flex as he paddled hard

and glided ahead of her. A small shiver attacked her spine as she recalled the way those muscles had flexed when she first came to after passing out, and began kissing him back. He had pulled her closer, and she had felt those hard arms under her back, lifting her body. . . .

Unnoticed, her paddle hung idle in the water as she remembered the way his lips had felt on hers, the taste of him, the scent of his skin. There had been something she couldn't identify, and it was intriguing. She wished she hadn't run away from him the night before. Maybe, if she'd stayed, she'd know now what it was, that elusive teasing taste. She closed her eyes, trying to conjure it up, then kept them closed, savoring the memory, projecting far into a series of what-ifs before she drew herself up short.

She had been kissed before, of course, but seldom had she spent so much time dwelling on those kisses and anticipating what they could lead to.

Even Antonio had been only a very close friend. What was so different this time?

This time? Hey, hold it, she told herself. You are not anticipating any more kisses with Cal Mixall, or anything else with him, for that matter, except looking after two mutual relatives.

"B.J.?"

"What?" Kara's voice startled her so much B.J. jumped, making the canoe rock alarmingly. Her niece clutched the gunwales, her paddle splashing into the lake, head turned toward her aunt, her eyes wide. She fished the child's paddle out of the water and passed it to her.

"Where did they go?" Kara asked.

"Who?"

"Uncle Cal and Laura. They're gone!"

B.J. blinked and blinked again, scanning the lake.

Where *had* Cal and Laura gone? One minute the other canoe was right there, traveling smoothly next to a stretch of reedy shore, and the next it had disappeared completely. She could see no splashing or waving paddles to indicate the other two might have capsized, but it was as if they had been swallowed whole.

"They can't be far away," she said. "They must have slipped into a creek mouth or something, or gone around a point that blends into the shore from here. We'll catch them soon."

Strongly now, she paddled, feeling the blade bite deep into the water, forcing it through, the pull in her arms and back and shoulders hard and unfamiliar. But it was a good feeling, and she thought she could have gone on like that for hours. The hard physical labor quelled those other feelings that had been coming too close to the surface.

Close to shore they skimmed, following the line the other canoe had been on. Yet as closely as she was watching, she would have missed them entirely if she hadn't heard Laura giggle.

"Laura? Where are you?" She backpaddled, bringing the canoe to a halt, then kept it still by feathering the blade gently as she peered at the foliage along the lakeshore.

"Right here. Can't you see us?"

"No, I . . . Oh!" She gasped when Laura's hand appeared in a small gap within the wall of vegetation. "My gosh! What a hideout!"

"Back up about six feet," said Cal's smooth voice, "and you'll see the entrance." B.J. wanted to paddle away hard and fast, seeking that delicious anticipation again, but Kara had caught onto some of the bushes and was forcing the canoe backward.

"It's one of Uncle Cal's blinds," Laura explained as Cal caught the bow of her canoe, guiding it into a narrow cut in the reeds where his own was nestled up against a small, decked raft. The raft was completely surrounded by six-foot-high wooden walls, with enough greenery around to render them invisible from even a few feet away. Under a lean-to roof at one end, Laura sat cross-legged on a platform two feet above the deck and about as wide as a double bed.

"Uncle Cal sleeps here sometimes," Laura said, "so he can get pictures and drawings of the birds when they come to feed at dawn. He can even make coffee," she added proudly, indicating a small propane stove on a table that hung from the wall near the foot of the bunk. B.J. noticed a length of rolled canvas hanging from the top of the lean-to room, which could be dropped to keep out rain and cold, making the bunk area very snug, like a small, private cave. Something atavistic stirred in her and she pushed it away.

"Just like a treehouse, isn't it?" Laura said as B.J. and Kara joined her and her uncle on the raft. It dipped slightly under the added weight, but then settled to bobbing gently with their movements.

"A treehouse," B.J. said, mostly to distract herself from thinking about camping out in this snug place—with the man who owned it. "That's what you kids could be doing while your uncle's busy. Why don't you build yourselves a treehouse?"

Cal lifted his brows. "Do girls like treehouses?"

"Girls love treehouses!" came a chorus of three voices.

He slowly shook his head. "Well, well, well. I think it's a very good thing you came, Great-Aunt Barbara. Maybe, if I keep you around, I'll learn more about the care and feeding of two young ladies, and how to make them happy while they're here."

"Aw, Uncle Cal, we're not really that unhappy, you

know," Kara said, hopping off the bunk and hugging him. "It's just that it's so much nicer having both you and B.J. here."

He hugged her back, then looked over at B.J., who was perched on the end of the sleeping platform with Laura. "I think so, too, punkin." He smiled, eyes half-hooded. "All I have to do now is think of some way to get her to stay."

Five

B.J. froze at the look on his face, then began to tremble deep inside. The trembling worsened when he set Kara back on her feet, checked the zipper of her orange life jacket, and said, "If you two want some canoe time, it's nice and sheltered at this end of the lake, so feel free. Laura, you in the stern. You're stronger." He held the canoe steady as the girls clambered in eagerly. Gently, Cal shoved them out past the reeds.

"You can go as far as that half-submerged log over there—the one with the bushes growing out of it—and then head back." He pointed to a strip of apparently floating shrubbery half a mile out into the lake.

Inexpertly, the girls moved the small craft along, but soon picked up a rhythm and paddled less jerkily, though still with much splashing.

A flock of ducks took to their wings with a lot of clatter, and B.J. shook her head. "You won't get much work done if this keeps up. They'll frighten off every living thing in the lake."

"The ducks will come back," he said easily, standing beside her as they watched the girls. "And I don't feel like working anyway." He tilted his head to one side and looked at her. "B.J., I meant what I said to Kara. I'd like you to stay. And there won't be any more antisocial behavior."

His words, for some reason, embarrassed her. What "antisocial behavior" was he referring to? His ill humor on Thursday, or his kisses last night? Since he'd already apologized for the former, she decided it had to be the latter.

"That's all right," she said, looking down. "I didn't take it seriously." If not with kisses, then how did he intend to persuade her to stay? Not that she was going to be persuaded, of course, but she wouldn't mind a few more kisses. She jumped, startled, when he tilted her face up, his fingers hard and warm under her chin, his other hand light on her waist.

"I wish you would take me seriously," he said softly. "I have such a hard time keeping my hands off you that I'm beginning to think I have a very serious problem where you're concerned."

So maybe he wasn't apologizing for kissing her. She knew she should pull back from him, but once more she was mesmerized by him, overwhelmed by his pure masculinity. It was a feeling she was unaccustomed to. With great force of will, she pulled out of his loose embrace.

"Sorry, but I seldom take anything seriously," she said as she returned to sit on the end of the bunk platform. "Except my job."

"Couldn't you see this as part of your job? I mean, the only reason you're not teaching right now is because of the school's troubles. Stay, B.J. Stay and teach the girls here." He pulled his deck chair close to her and sank down onto its creaking seat. "Listen, by now you must have figured out that I like you, B.J. I find you more than just attractive." He lifted a hand as if to touch her, then dropped it back to his lap. "But if you aren't interested, I'll leave you alone. No matter what you decide about me, I really do want you to stay, if only for the girls' sake."

"I . . . can't, Cal. Remember? I'm house-sitting."

"It's not just that, is it? It's me." He blew out a gusty sigh. "I wish you'd tell me why you dislike me so! If you did, maybe I could fix it. It can't be something I've ever done to you because I can't even remember having met you, though Melody tells me I did."

A sudden look of consternation flooded his face. "Oh, no! Is that it? Is it because I *don't* remember you?"

B.J. had to laugh in spite of the confused emotions roiling within her. "Of course not. Heavens, I don't expect everyone I've ever met to remember me. Besides," she added uncomfortably, "I was probably too young to make much of an impression."

He looked at her meditatively. "You were eighteen. A guy of twenty-three, if he was anywhere near normal, would remember someone who must have looked like you did at eighteen." He laughed softly. "Especially someone who was, at eighteen, an aunt to the twenty-two-year-old bride."

"We seldom told people I was her aunt. It embarrassed both of us, I guess. So people just assumed I was another cousin. There were . . . there were a lot of teenage cousins running around that weekend," she said quickly, wanting only to get off this subject. "You can't be expected to remember all of us."

"Do you remember me?"

Her quiet, "Yes," was among the greatest understatements she'd ever made. "After all, you were the best man." *And she had been asked to be maid of honor, but had declined.* Both Melody and Phyllis had been angry with her over that. Now, even more than before, she was glad she'd been firm in her refusal. An ugly maid of honor, he'd have remembered, for sure.

"I'm not surprised you remember me," he said.

"I'm sure you're not," she said dryly. "Women don't usually forget Cal Mixall, do they?"

He winced. "That wasn't the way I meant it. I recall being such a snot that weekend, it's surprising everyone who was there doesn't remember me with horror."

Drawing a series of circles on his knee with the tip of one finger, he went on, "I was a real pain in the . . . rear to everyone that weekend, I'm told." He looked up, fixing her with his dark eyes. "Is that why you hate me, B.J.?"

She laughed softly. "Cal, I don't hate you. I don't know you. And when I told the kids I didn't like you, I was simply making a point. Can't you forget I ever said it?"

"I'd like to, but I can't as long as I still get the feeling it's true."

"All right, Cal. I like you. Better?"

"Much," he said, but he frowned. Maybe she had only said it to placate him.

"Why were you so gloomy at the wedding?" she asked. Twelve years ago she had been too timid to ask, but she had wondered. Phyllis had assumed he was having woman problems, but B.J. had thought that unlikely. How could a man as handsome as he not have any woman he wanted?

"I'd just got my bachelor's degree in fine arts, and had been accepted to study under Piet Van Hoek, the portrait painter." He looked off into the distance, remembering.

Into his silence, B.J. said encouragingly, "I've seen some of his work. I taught a class on modern artists a couple of years ago. He doesn't—didn't—take on many private students, I think I remember reading." She was impressed and didn't try to hide it. "You must have been very, very good, even then." She hesitated, wondering if this could be considered prying. "I didn't know you did portraits."

"I don't," he said curtly, and she saw a flash of pain in his eyes before he looked down again at the finger continuing its little circles on his knee. After a moment he looked up again, eyes tormented. "I thought I could, you know. I really did. But Piet taught me different. I thought I was good, too. But I wasn't."

"Oh, Cal, that can't be true." Impulsively, she reached out a hand to him, clasping her fingers around his. "I mean, look how successful you are."

"But I'm not what I want to be, dammit!" His voice was harsh and his fingers tightened painfully on hers. "Where's the success in that?

"Sorry," he said after a moment, loosening his grip on her. She pulled her hand back onto her lap. "I didn't mean to hurt you." He drove his long fingers through his dark hair, brushing it back off his forehead. "Back then," he went on, "when I was a young graduate, I had a highly inflated opinion of my own worth, especially when Van Hoek accepted me as one of his students. I wanted to be a portrait painter like him. And that's all I wanted. You're right. He didn't take many of us."

"And this made you gloomy?"

His smile was sardonic as he shook his head. "Oh, no. When I learned that I'd been accepted, I was out of my mind with glee. I was good, damned good, and I knew it. I was also insufferably cocky, and went to him with the attitude that *he* was lucky to have *me*."

He grimaced. "That old Dutchman did some mighty quick attitude adjustment on me, let me tell you. He cut me into such fine shreds that I could have been boiled up and served as linguine. In twenty-five minutes, he proved to me that I knew nothing, was nothing, and was probably incapable of ever becoming anything other than a hack who painted pretty pictures of bowls of fruit that would be copied en masse and sold at Woolco on dollar-forty-nine day. And he sent me away. Until I could grow up and become a man, as he put it. Hell, I thought I'd been a man for years.

"I was still smarting from that when Curt got married. In fact, my interview with old Piet came just hours before we were due to fly out here for the wedding. It wasn't easy to learn such a lesson, and it put me in a lousy frame of mind for what was supposed to be a festive occasion. It took me several weeks to assimilate it fully, and to become humble enough to go back to him and beg for a second chance, because I knew that without his tutelage, I would be exactly what he said, a nothing, going nowhere. I worked with him for seven years, until he died. And I learned how to paint. But never like him," he added with quiet despair. "Never portraits."

"Maybe that's good," she said quietly after a few minutes, when he failed to go on. "It would have been a shame if you were just another Piet Van Hoek."

"Why do you say that? He was certainly worth emulating."

"Because you are so far from being a nothing, going nowhere, that it would have been a great loss if you hadn't become what you are. You must miss your friend terribly."

"Yes." He looked at her with surprise. "How did you know he was my friend?"

"Because when you mention his name, your eyes go soft."

Cal looked startled. "Do they?" He laughed shortly. "I loved him, you know. And I never told him. I wonder if he knew?" His eyes filled with such misery, she reached out to him again. He accepted the clasp of her hand as he went on, smoothing his thumb over her knuckles. "Piet was very special to me, B.J., but like all of his students, I pretended to scorn him for his old-fashioned ways, his insistence that we learn the basics before we learned anything else. We thought we knew the basics. After all, most of us had been taking art lessons all our lives, and had university degrees. But he was such a good man, as well as a genius, and you're right, I do miss him terribly."

Suddenly he looked away from her, snatching his hand back. He pounded a fist on his thigh. "Oh, hell!" he said, sniffling loudly. "What's the matter with me? What have you done, B.J. Gray? Cast a spell over me or something?"

"I'm not the type to cast spells," she said dismissively, getting to her feet. She shaded her eyes as she watched the girls, now on their way back from the floating garden, more to give Cal time to recover than because she was concerned for the children. They were paddling easily now, fluidly, cooperating with each other, but still she watched them.

She knew Cal was uncomfortable about revealing weakness in front of her, and she wanted to give him time to regather his forces. When he spoke her name softly, she turned around and he was just . . . there, looking at her with something in his eyes that sent her heart rate soaring.

Her mouth went dry. She wanted to move away, but something held her there. His eyes. They had that kind of power over her. They were gazing into hers, dark, watchful, then he lifted one hand to touch her hair. It was a feather-light touch, but she felt it right to the soles of her feet. She shivered as he slowly slid his fingers through her hair, then clamped his hand around her head, drawing her toward him.

If his kiss had been meant as one of thanks, it changed subtly as she returned it, roughening, though not unpleasantly, as he sought something more from her. What it was, she didn't know, and wasn't sure she was giving it, or was even capable of giving it. His lips moved over hers beseechingly, and she strained against him, stroking his tongue with her own, clinging to him as her arms went around his waist and her breasts flattened against his hard chest. Her knees grew weak, and she clutched at his shirt as her head swam with the dizziness of pleasure. Heat coursed through her, making her tremble, and again she tasted that elusive, unique flavor of him and was intrigued beyond measure.

"Ah, B.J.," he said moments later, holding her head with both hands, pressing her forehead to his chest as if afraid to look into her eyes. "You are so the type to cast spells."

And so was he, she thought. And so strong was the spell over both of them, they didn't move apart until the girls' voices alerted them that they wouldn't be alone much longer. Cal stepped back half a pace and bent, dropping a light kiss onto the tip of her nose. Then he let her go, trailing his hands down her arms until he touched only the fingers of one hand, staring down into her eyes, still searching.

B.J. was the one who looked away first. "I think we should go," she said. "It's getting chilly." How, she wondered, had she come up with that when a tingling warmth had flushed her skin from her toes up, and all because of Cal Mixall's words, and Cal Mixall's voice, and Cal Mixall's eyes?

"Yes," he said, reluctantly allowing the tips of her fingers to slide out of his grasp as the girls' canoe poked its bow through the reeds toward his little shelter. "Can you take both the kids with you?"

B.J. looked up at him as she crouched, holding the gunwale of the canoe. "Yes, of course."

"I . . . think I'd better stay here for a while. And get some work done," he added almost as an afterthought.

She stared into his expressionless eyes for another moment, then nodded and got into the stern of the canoe. Laura was in the bow with the other paddle and Kara was in the middle.

"Hey," Cal said softly. She looked up. "I'll see you later, okay?"

She nodded and looked away again, gently shoving the canoe out of the blind. When she glanced back, Cal was spreading his sleeping bag open on the bunk and she wondered just how long he intended to stay there. He didn't look at her again, but took out a sketchpad and pencil and moved toward one of the small viewports, seemingly oblivious to their departure.

A faint sound drew B.J. from her tumbled bed to the window of her room. Her gaze swept the lake, searching for whatever it was that had disturbed her. Ah! There. Of course.

The scene was slightly blurred because she didn't have her contacts in, but blurred or not, it was still a dreamy, romantic sight with the silver of the moon track laid out across the lake and the black silhouette of man and canoe clearly outlined as Cal paddled homeward. She sighed and felt a deep sense of satisfaction as she watched him approach. Her sleeplessness, she admitted, had been for one reason only: she had been waiting for Cal to come home.

He was still a long way out, but coming closer, his powerful arms and shoulders working smoothly as he drove his paddle into the water and stroked it back. The rhythm of his body in motion caught and increased the rhythm of the blood in her veins, and the restlessness within her soul translated itself to a deep and elemental longing.

Lord, but he disturbed her, even seen dimly in moonlight. Or maybe it was because of the moonlight. Maybe it was that which had infiltrated her senses, stolen her resistance to the memory of his kisses, to the yearning for more of them. For more . . .

All evening, it had plagued her, this new and unfamiliar restlessness that welled up within her. After the girls had gone to bed, she had paced from room to room, examining all of his paintings, remembering his passion as he spoke of his swans. She'd searched for the same element in all his paintings, and found it, feeling somehow that she was discovering the man behind the work.

She thought back on their every conversation, reliving each word, each nuance, remembering the throb in his voice when he said he couldn't keep his hands off her. It was insane, but she felt the same way about him. Him, Calvin Mixall! The last man in the world she'd have ever expected to feel this way about.

This way . . .

What, exactly, was "this way"? What was she feeling? What did it mean? Her very soul cried out for something she couldn't quite name. Now, seeing Cal out there, paddling toward her across the silver lake, she discovered she could name it with no difficulty at all.

A mate. Someone of her very own. But . . . him?

Why, of all the men she'd met, was he the first one to stir her this deeply, to make her yearn for love and marriage and a family of her own? Was it real, this enormous feeling in her heart? Was it love? Or was it simply the residue of a very brief, and very foolish, girlhood infatuation with a fascinating stranger? She gripped the curtains tightly. It had to be the latter. It simply had to be! She couldn't be so foolish as to have fallen in love—even a little way in love—with Cal Mixall.

Yet shouldn't she forgive him that careless laughter twelve years ago? Because, hadn't she looked like a life raft? Of course she had, and her face had been pocked, scarred with acne . . . and now Cal Mixall liked her skin. He'd stroked his fingers over her cheek and said, "You have the most beautiful skin."

He liked, too, the hair that had once been mousy brown, and the eyes that had caused so many comments as she grew up. One gray, one green, they gave a lopsided, gargoyle look, especially when teamed with that awful nose stuck in the middle of her fat face like a blob of plasticene. He had, just today, kissed her nose, never knowing that it wasn't as it had once been. She shivered, stroking her own fingers where his had moved, wondering why, with his keen artist's eye, he wasn't seeing the truth when he looked at her.

As she watched, he stepped out of the canoe onto the wharf. Bending, he grasped the bow of the slender craft and with one heave brought it half onto the wharf. Then, taking a long pace back, he drew the canoe completely out of the water in a graceful, sweeping motion. Taking his pack from the bottom of it, he turned the boat upside down, hitched the strap of the pack over one shoulder, and strode toward the house.

She froze. Was it her imagination, or did his face turn toward the window where she stood?

Did he see her? If he knew she was awake, watching for him to return, would he come to her door and speak to her? Her heart hammered hard at the thought. If he did, what would he say? And if he did, what would she do?

She remained very still, not daring to move, and when he walked on by, she could see that his head was lowered and his walk weary. He looked, she thought, totally preoccupied. No, he hadn't looked at her window. He probably wasn't even aware, at the moment, that she was in his house. When he was out of sight, she let the curtains fall back into place and returned to bed.

But not to sleep.

• • • •

Cal looked at the darkened house, scanning the windows as he walked up the path from the float.

Damn! She'd gone to bed.

He frowned. Well, why not? After all it was late. But he'd said, "See you later," hadn't he? She should have known he hadn't meant to spend the entire night in the blind. He'd only stayed late enough for the full moon to come up—the harvest moon—so he could take some time exposures of the lake at night. If it hadn't been for Laura and Kara, he'd have invited her to join him in the blind. He grimaced. If it weren't for Laura and Kara, she'd never have come there in the first place.

He wished she were with him now in the chilly night air, breathing in the faint scent of wood smoke from Fred's chimney, the pungency of evergreens, and the faintly musty smell of fallen leaves, gazing out over the moon-drenched lake. She would shiver at the hint of frost in the air, and he would wrap her in his arms and warm her. Ah, B.J. . . . What a woman she was! She'd cast such a spell over him that one minute he didn't think he was going to break free, and the next, didn't want to.

He smiled to himself and looked again at her window. He nearly halted, but forced himself to keep on walking in the same slow, measured pace, not to let on that he'd seen that pale face and form and her shimmery hair bracketed by two sweeps of curtain. She was still awake! She was standing in her window watching him come home!

His pleasure was a living thing within his chest. As he'd made the long trip home through the moonlight, he'd been thinking how wonderful it would be to find her waiting up for him. And she was. At least she was awake. That was something.

Gently, he knocked on her door. There was no

reply. Frowning, he knocked again. She couldn't be asleep already. It hadn't been three minutes since he'd seen her at her window, awake—thinking about him?—just as he'd thought of her all the way back down the lake.

"B.J.?" No reply. "Could I talk to you?"

The silence from the other side of her door was profound. At length, he sighed and turned away, returning to his own side of the house.

He climbed into bed and stretched the aching muscles his shower hadn't eased. He was exhausted. He yearned for sleep, for the oblivion of it, but the more he sought it, the more it eluded him.

An hour later he got up, pulled on his jeans again, and stomped into his studio. If he couldn't sleep, he might as well work—if he could. Ten minutes after arriving in his studio, he threw his brush down angrily. Just as he seldom had trouble sleeping, he seldom had trouble concentrating on work—until now. She distracted him. Bewitched him. He wished he could get her out of his mind. He wished he didn't remember her passionate kisses, her cornsilk colored hair, her satiny skin.

He stared at the nearly finished painting on his easel for a long time, dissatisfied. He continued to consider it as he mixed paints, but even as he worked his mind was only half on it. Absently, he stroked a few flecks of dark green into the pewter sky. With his knife, he scraped it off. It was wrong. There was something . . . something he couldn't quite see, and he wished the Dutchman were there to tell him where he was going wrong.

Cal groaned, shaking his head as he remembered what had happened at the blind. He couldn't believe he'd bared his soul like that in front of B.J. Her compassion and sympathy had been geniune. *Oh, dammit, woman, get out of my mind!* he said silently, still staring at the painting, but not seeing it. Concentrate, he told himself. Pay attention to your work. He stepped back another pace, as Piet would have done, tilted his head to the side. No. Nothing. No new insight.

A new insight . . . The words echoed in his mind for a moment before he recognized them. Of course! With a sense of relief, he remembered something he had once seen his mentor do. He had asked why at the time, but the old man had just shrugged. "A different perspective can provide a new insight."

As he'd watched Piet, Cal had seen no difference, but clearly the other man had, because he had gone on to create one of the most brilliant portraits the world had seen. And what had worked for Piet might well work for Cal, even though this wasn't a portrait. Except . . . in a way, it was. It just wasn't a portrait of a human being.

Carefully lifting the canvas from the easel, he carried it out of his studio and into his bedroom. After a moment, he realized it wasn't going to work. Someone else had to hold the canvas.

This wasn't just an excuse, he told himself. He genuinely needed assistance. And as the only other person who might be awake, B.J. was the only one who could provide it.

He knocked on her door again, and again got no reply. He opened the door quietly. She was sitting up, staring at him, the sheet clutched under her chin, her eyes wide. As he flipped the switch by the door she raised a hand quickly to shield her eyes and looked at him from under its dark shadow.

"What's wrong?" Her voice was not husky with sleep, he thought in triumph. She had been awake all this time, just as he had.

He drew in a deep breath, conscious of the sweet smell, the warm, tantalizing woman-scent emanating from her bed, but willed himself not to be distracted now. Not to be distracted? In the same room as this woman—with a bed? Hah! "I need . . . help."

She frowned. Why hadn't he said so earlier, she wondered, instead of just coming to her door and saying he wanted to talk? She'd lain there, rigid, torn between wanting to get up and go to him, and wanting him to go away. She'd told herself it was relief making her shake when he'd finally done just that. "Help?" she said. "With what?"

He breathed out heavily, making an effort to concentrate. "You'll have to get up and come with me," he said tautly. "Please?"

She took her hand down, looked at him through a shutter of lashes as if the light were still too bright. "Where? Why?" At least he didn't want this "help" here in her bedroom. She was grateful for that.

"I need you to hold a canvas for me. Just for a minute or two. Please. It's important, B.J., or I wouldn't have disturbed you."

His voice throbbed faintly, and she almost looked at him fully but caught herself in time. Two-tone eyes. If he saw them, surely he'd remember fat, ugly Janie. *You have the most beautiful blue eyes. . . .* She stiffened as if he had just said the words aloud.

"Please," he said once more, and she nodded.

"All right, but give me a couple of minutes." *What are you doing?* she asked herself with desperation. There was no answer, and she glanced at him again as he hesitated in her doorway. It was impossible not to notice his bare shoulders and chest, and just as impossible not to respond to them. His hair, so dark it looked almost blue, was tousled, as if he'd been in bed.

You are out of your mind, she told herself two minutes later, standing in the bathroom, blinking to rid her eyes of the tears caused by her lens solution. Lock your door. Go back to bed. Better yet, go out to that shed, get on your bike, and hightail it out of here, fast, B.J. Fast!

She wasn't dressed when she came out of her room, Cal saw, though the time she'd taken, she could have changed six times. Her hair had been brushed and she wore a knee-length white terry robe belted tightly around her slim middle, the lace trim of a yellow nightgown visible between the lapels. An involuntary smile of delight curved his mouth, then a surge of heat struck his loins as he stared down at her bare feet.

They were so small, so slender, so . . . Dammit, she had the cutest little feet and the sexiest toes! That was crazy. He'd never before seen anything erotic about women's feet, yet hers, with their toenails polished pale pink to match her fingernails, were sexier than anything he'd ever seen before. He knew he was in danger of forgetting himself, but he fought down his desire, buried it deep within, telling himself to get his mind back on his work.

There was nothing sexy about toes! There never had been and there never would be. He was overtired and worried about his painting, and for that reason he was overreacting. It had nothing to do with her smelling like a garden of wildflowers, earthy and sweet, but still he wanted to hold her, kiss her, and wanted to do a lot of other things to her, and— *Dammit, cut that out!* he told himself sharply, swinging open the door to his room. "In here," he said, wondering if he'd follow anyone who barked like that at him in the middle of the night.

Six

B.J. followed Cal, wondering why she didn't just tell him to take his ill humor and paddle it back down to the other end of the lake. Then she halted abruptly in the doorway when she realized he'd led her to his bedroom, not his studio.

"Excuse me, but is this necess—" She broke off, realizing he was intent on a painting propped against the foot of his bed. As far as he was concerned, the painting was the important item in the room, not the bed. She doubted if he was half as aware of the bed as she was. Determined to be as detached from the sight of that huge expanse of tumbled sheets and blankets, from the sensations it sent through her body, she asked, "You want me to hold that?"

"Please," he said. "I have to get back from it to gain the right perspective. Put your hands down in front of you and turn them over . . . palms out."

He placed the painting in her arms. Her fingers wrapped gingerly just over the bottom edge of the canvas as she tilted her head back to make room for it to rest under her chin.

"Great," he said. "Now, turn this way. Face the mirror. Good. Hold still."

They both looked, she with curiosity, he with a depth of concentration that told her she hardly existed to him at the moment. She bit back a wry smile. So much for her worries. She was an easel, one that could be positioned correctly, she realized as he turned her an inch to one side, then tilted her forward a bit. He stepped back and gazed into the mirror at the image of his painting.

It was an eagle standing on a gnarled limb, the darkness of a pewter sky behind, an angry slate of water below, with rolling clouds and wind-whipped trees conveying a sense of impending doom that made goose bumps dot her arms. Something, the bird, maybe, but perhaps just the general tone of the painting, was threatening. Then she saw it. On a narrow strip of brown, wintery land edged by icy water, a small creature—a mouse?—hid under a leaf. The viewer had to guess whether the bird knew it was there and was about to attack, or if the little rodent was safe—for the moment. It was a menacing picture in one way, yet one in which she could find hope. It made her want to ask, "Who wins?" and she knew she was cheering for the mouse.

"That's it," Cal said softly, the tension seeping out of him. "There it is." He smiled. Not at her, but at the painting, at . . . a ghost? she wondered when he whispered, "Thanks, Piet."

"There what is?" she asked as he took the canvas from her. She rubbed her arms.

"What I couldn't see. It was all in the bird's expression. It was too . . . passive. I wasn't able to convey its hunger, its ferocity and need. But now I think I can."

"Could I . . . could I watch?" she surprised herself by asking.

"Sure." He smiled and gestured for her to leave first. As they entered his studio B.J. wondered what in the world she was doing there at half-past one in

the morning when she should be asleep. But nothing, she knew, would have stopped her being with
him just then. She was fascinated, not only by what
he was doing, but by the man himself. She knew
she was risking much, yet she wanted to be with
him, to learn more about him.

B.J. had never been in a working artist's studio
before, and was amazed at the brightness of the lights
and by the clutter. How could he work in such chaos?
Stretched canvases leaned haphazardly against walls,
in corners, on shelves. Paintings in various stages
of completion stood here and there; tubes and pots
and brushes and oddly shaped implements littered a
long counter. From that clutter, Cal picked up a
tube of paint, scrutinized its label, set it down again.
He chose another, contemplated it while chewing
his bottom lip, then nodded. He squirted a glob of it
onto a palette, mixed a tiny dab from a different
tube, then faced the easel.

Picking up a fine brush, he added a touch of those
mixed red shades to the gleaming yellow eye of the
eagle, then changed brushes and dabbed in some
smoky gray. Suddenly there was an impression of
hooded violence that hadn't been there before.

Incredulous, B.J. leaned forward. Never had she
seen so vast a difference made with only a few flicks
of a paintbrush.

"How did you do that? I mean, how did you know
to do exactly what you did?"

He gave her a quick smile over his shoulder. "I
can't tell you how I knew to do it," he said as he
continued to work, using a different brush this time,
and another color, touching up the underside of a
branch of a tree. "I just did. But I couldn't see it
before, until I got that new perspective."

"Backward?" she asked, intrigued. "In the mirror?"

"Yes. It's a trick I once saw my teacher use. I
couldn't see what he saw when he did it, but I knew

there was something going wrong with this, and I thought it wouldn't hurt to try it. When I saw it reflected, I saw that it was in the bird itself where the soul of the painting must lie. I had thought I could achieve it purely through the anger of the water, the menace of the sky."

"But you did," she said, walking away from him, so that she could no longer see the painting, but could see his face. She sat on the one chair the room offered, curling her legs up beside her, watching him paint. She forgot that she didn't want to be fascinated by him. She forgot everything but being there with him, watching his large, competent hand holding the brush with such delicacy. The intensity of his eyes, shadowed by his heavy dark brows, was thrilling to see—as long as it was directed toward his work and in no way threatening her. His mouth was firm and chiseled, held straight as he worked, but now and then twisting to one side or the other as if he was considering something. He bit his lower lip, tilted his head, then shot a sidelong glance at her, telling her that he hadn't forgotten her presence.

"I did what?"

She hadn't wanted him to talk, to notice her. She wanted to watch him work for the rest of the night, the week, her life. . . . She brought her thoughts to a quick halt and said, "You made the threat so real it almost terrified me, made me feel as if I were under attack. Until I saw the mouse, and then when I did, I wanted it to be safe. I thought it was."

He looked startled and pleased as he turned to face her fully. "You saw that? I thought the mouse was a detail that the viewer would become aware of only slowly, after seeing the menace."

"I saw the menace first, believe me. It wasn't until I looked more closely that I saw what was being menaced. And now . . . now that you've changed it

. . ." Her voice trailed away, and he thought she was too polite to say what she really felt.

"Now that I've changed it . . . what?" he asked softly, leaving the painting. He crouched before her, his hands on the arms of the wicker chair, his eyes intent on hers. "Do you like it better the way it is now? Or the way it was then?"

She felt, for just a moment, like a mouse, and wished she had a leaf to hide under.

"Now," she said in a faintly tremulous voice, "I can see that the eagle knows where the mouse is, and is just . . . waiting, and . . ."

"And?"

"And the eagle is going to swoop at any moment."

Cal heard the quaver in her voice and noticed that her breathing was slightly ragged. He noticed, too, that crazy little pulse in her throat.

"You don't want it to?" he asked. Her answer, he knew, was of great importance, that they weren't just talking about a painting now.

She shook her head, and he held his breath as golden fire shot from her hair into his eyes, dazzling him. "I . . . don't know," she said. "Part of me wants it to. And part of me fears for the mouse."

"If I told you there was nothing to fear?" he asked, dropping one hand to where her feet were tucked up beside her. He covered them with the warmth of his clasp and still felt her shiver.

Her laugh was breathless. "Nothing to fear? The mouse is going to be devoured."

He smiled. "But what if the mouse recognizes that as its . . . destiny? What if it wants what is going to happen because it knows it will go on to another, maybe better, plane of existence?"

"You're getting too—too metaphysical for me."

His chuckle was warm, as warm as the hand on her feet. "You'd prefer me to get physical, instead?"

"No." She said the word, but there was so little

conviction in her voice that neither of them gave it much credence.

"Why not? What if I told you that you, like the mouse, have nothing to fear?"

B.J. drew in a sharp breath. What was he doing? Why was he stroking her ankle like that? It was as bad—no, worse—than when he'd touched her face and neck when they'd kissed. And just as good. "Maybe I wouldn't be able to believe you," she said, forcing herself to meet his gaze.

"Why not?" he said again.

"Because you, like the eagle, are a predator."

His hand encircled one of her ankles, and he pulled gently, drawing her foot out to rest on his knee. Reaching out a long arm, he plucked a clean paint-brush from a nearby shelf, then stroked its feather-soft tip from her arch to her toes.

"Predators have needs," he murmured. He lifted her foot and placed his lips on the toes he had just stroked. Glancing up at her wide, startled eyes, he said, "I wanted to do that today, when you came over to my side of the argument with Laura. I want to tell you how much that meant."

She licked her lips. "You . . . thanked me quite nicely then."

He lightly brushed her instep with those soft bris-tles, then followed up with a strong, steady pressure of his fingers. She felt heat begin to rise in delicate spirals all the way up her leg to the top of her thigh. It took up residence in the lower part of her belly and she quivered, her toes curling on his thigh.

"Cal . . ."

The brush made tiny circles as it traced a path up her calf, flicked in behind her knee, and then ap-proached the hem of her robe. "What?" He didn't look at her, intent on following the trail of the paint-brush up her leg.

"Stop." It was a hoarse little sound, and at that, he did look up, his eyes unsmiling, dark, hungry.

He reversed the brush, and reversed its direction, drawing the pointed handle from her thigh back to her foot, slowly, teasingly, right out to the tip of her big toe. Gently, he placed her foot on the floor and she lowered the other one to cross over it, rubbing, trying to negate the tingling sensations that continued to race across her skin.

He sat back on his heels, letting his hands dangle between his knees, the brush swaying from side to side as he held it between finger and thumb. Then, smiling at her, he got to his feet and held out a hand to help her up. For a moment they stood close together. She felt the heat emanating from his body, saw the hunger in his eyes, and knew that he must be reading the same in hers. Her cheeks were flushed, and she wished her skin didn't always betray her so.

How had it happened? she wondered. Where had it sprung from, this mutual wanting of theirs? And where would it lead? With just a look, just a touch, he could make her crave things she knew she was better off not having. Not when wanting them meant needing him in order to get them. If this was what falling in love was all about, then she wasn't certain she wanted to go on with it.

"Cal . . . I think I'd better go."

"Please, not yet," he said, and caught her upper arms in those large, competent hands. They held her, she thought dimly, as delicately as they held a paintbrush, but then her thinking apparatus went completely on the fritz because he was kissing her.

The warmth of his lips overwhelmed her, beguiled her, and she parted hers for the inquiring tip of his tongue, her senses filled with him. There it was again, that scent, that taste, and she wanted desperately to know what it was because it was his. She ached to be closer to him, to press her body to his, because maybe, her whirling mind thought, in greater closeness she would be able to name what was just on the edge of her consciousness. A delicious, quivery, wonderful feeling stole over her as she lifted her hands and placed them on his bare chest, running them up the narrow strip of silky hair that widened toward his collarbone.

The hard jut of one pebblelike nipple came under the tip of her finger, and she pressed experimentally, feeling him shudder in response. His mouth hardened over hers as his hands tightened on her arms, holding her back from him. She ached deep inside, wanting to be closer, but he continued to hold her away, keeping her several tantalizing inches from the full embrace she yearned for. When she felt one of his knees brush between hers, sliding in at the hem of her robe, she swayed, rubbing her burning skin against the smooth denim. He caught her against him, bending her head back as his arms swept fully around her. At the strength of his embrace, she moaned, and he lifted his head at once.

"I did it again," he said hoarsely. "I said I wouldn't do that, and yet I did. Twice. And I hurt you."

She shook her head, breathing out a soft denial, but she couldn't look at him. Her chest was heaving and her heart hurt with the force of its hammering, but he hadn't caused her any pain. Except by breaking that kiss so abruptly.

"We were both . . . involved in it," she said.

"Involved? That's a good choice of word. When I touch you, something primitive happens to me." He captured her arms again, his thumbs making little circles on the sleeves of her robe. "Total involvement." Within the confines of the heavy terry cloth, her nipples were as taut as if those thumbs were circling there. Slowly, she lifted her gaze to his face and just looked.

"Ah, B.J."

Cal drew her tightly against him, rocking her from side to side, and tangled one hand in the back of her hair. He smiled into her eyes and saw hunger there, but fear, too. He suspected it was the same kind of fear he felt; fear that maybe this was too big, too unmanageable. If he had any sense, he'd get her out of his life before it was too late, but he didn't think he could stop what was happening, or that he wanted to. The intensity of what she could make him feel was foreign to him, yet even though he knew he should proceed with caution, the very unfamiliarity of it made him want to explore it to the end.

So why was he standing here, looking at her, and not embarking on that exploration? Because there was something about B.J. that warned him she wasn't as sophisticated as most women at the age of thirty. A woman with her looks must have attracted men like nectar did bees, but she didn't act like a woman who knew how to handle such attentions. Nor did she kiss as if she had spent the last ten years or so exchanging embraces with willing men. Why it was so, how it could be so, eluded him, but long ago he'd learned to listen to his instincts. Right now they were screaming at him, *Go easy!*

Only, how could he, when he wanted her so much? But he wanted, also, to reassure her.

"You're afraid of me, I think," he said, sliding his hand around her cheek as he gazed into those blue, blue eyes. "Don't be, B.J. I'm not the predator you think I am."

She met his gaze, a tiny, forced smile curving her lips. "Aren't you? I think you are."

Though he shook his head in denial, he knew that in many ways her assessment was true. Or had been, once. But that was a long time ago. He liked to think he'd not only learned discretion, but had acquired patience and a lot more integrity since the days of his youthful excesses.

"All right," he said finally. "I guess I sometimes acted like a predator in the past. Or maybe I simply took what was freely offered and didn't look any further. I don't really know. I've never analyzed it. I just know that things are . . . different now."

"Why?" she asked. The tinge of bitterness in her tone made him frown. "Why should anything be different this time?"

He lifted one hand and ran it over the tumble of curls on her forehead. "Just . . . because. Because I think they are." His fingertips trailed to the tip of her nose and down across her lips, over her chin to her throat. "And you know what else I think?"

Her heart beat high and fast in her throat. "What else?"

He continued to let his finger travel, its hard tip tracing a line along her collarbone, just until the yellow lace peeking from her lapel stopped it. She shivered deep inside, wishing the lace, the lapel, weren't there to stop his wandering hand, and wishing he didn't have the power to make her want him so badly. He didn't want the same things from life she wanted, and even if he did, he wouldn't want them with her.

"I think," he murmured, "you feel the same way about me as I do about you, even though it might scare you a bit." He smiled, and his finger found its way under the lace, easing down from her collarbone to the upper curve of breast. "So why don't you stay? I think we'd both enjoy finding out just how well we could learn to . . . like each other."

"No." It was barely a faint breath, but he seemed to hear it, and to hear the determination in it, because his smile faded.

"Why not?" he asked, looking into her eyes.

From somewhere, she found the strength to back away from him. He wasn't holding her tightly, and his hands fell to his sides.

"Because you aren't even thinking about us 'liking' each other," she said with quiet dignity. "You're thinking about getting me into your bed, and that's all this conversation is about. You don't know me, or want to know me. You don't care about me as a human being. I'm fresh female territory you haven't yet explored."

"That's getting pretty close to insulting," he warned her, and B.J. looked down.

Oh, Lord, what was she saying? Did she really believe that? She didn't know, she knew only that what he wanted from her was not merely tenderness and companionship. And that wasn't what she wanted from him, either. But what was he offering her? Was he, like the men she had met during her year as children's entertainment supervisor for Club Caribbean, simply out for what he could get and damn the consequences?

But was Cal necessarily as unscrupulous as some of those men had been? It didn't matter, because she was still unsure of herself.

"I'm sorry," she said finally. "But are you denying it?"

"No," he said, struggling against the anger her words provoked. What gave her the right to make such a sweeping, judgmental statement about him? But if they were to get anywhere, he was going to have to be up-front with her. "I do want to go to bed with you, but I want to know you in other ways, too. Is it so impossible that I could want both?"

"I think so." Why she thought that, she couldn't have said. After all, didn't she herself want both? Was it really so strange to think that he might, too? Yes. Because he was who he was. Or who she thought he was. Had thought. Oh, lordy, she didn't know what she thought anymore!

"B.J., I want you in every way that it's possible for a man to want a woman," he said softly, and his forthright manner rang true even to her skeptical ears. "But I promise I won't push you. I will, however, keep on trying to change your mind."

"Why?" she demanded, the agony of her confusion evident in her voice, in her bewildered eyes. "Why are you doing this? I'm not your kind of woman." A disgusted man had said that to her once, when she had panicked like, as he had put it, *a virginal twelve-year-old.* "Stick to the ones you're used to, and who are used to you, Cal. I'm not for you."

"I think you are," he said with dogged persistence. So much for not pushing, he thought, but dammit, he had to try to get through to her. This was important, and it wasn't a joke.

He stepped close to her again and touched her face. He had to do it. His hand wouldn't stay away, he ached so much to feel her skin against his fingers, against his palm. He cupped her cheek and chin, keeping her face turned to him. "And as to why," he went on huskily, deliberately holding her gaze, "you are the most beautiful woman I've ever met, and yet there's a purity about you, a cleanliness, a wholesome . . . goodness, that draws me to you. And I want you more than I can say."

She looked at him for a long time, then closed her eyes as if in pain. Her mouth twisted and she turned her head to one side as he gathered her close, wanting to comfort her, to make better whatever he had said to hurt her.

After a moment, she placed her palms on his chest and tipped her head back to look at him. She lifted her thick lashes and said, "Cal, look at me! Really *see* me! I am not beautiful. What you're seeing is an illusion."

He cradled her face between his hands and laughed softly as he dropped a kiss on her nose. "B.J., in spite of what you might think, you just happen to be totally gorgeous."

She stepped away from him carefully, as if there were mines on the floor all around him, then turned at the door to look back. "Good night, Cal. And . . . thank you."

Then she left.

Cal stood thinking bleak thoughts for several minutes before forcing himself to turn back to his easel. He stared at the painting, satisfied, or nearly so. Too bad other problems couldn't be solved "through a glass, darkly" or by the sweep of a sable brush, the flick of a palette knife. Or, he thought, turning from the easel and picking up a sketchpad, the turn of a pencil line.

He sat on the chair where B.J. had been, pad on his knee, and stared at the pencil lines his hand was drawing. Curves, angles, spirals. Curve of cheek, angle of shoulder and neck, spiral of shimmering hair on brow and temple. He flipped the page and drew some more, over and over, searching his memory for each mood he had seen on her mobile face, each change in her expressive eyes. Then, in frustration, he flung the sketchpad to the floor and buried his face in his hands.

Why couldn't he accept what he was? Accept his own limitations? He did. He had. For years he had known that he was an excellent painter of animal forms, but not of portraits, as he'd once aspired to be. And he had learned not to let it matter. So why was it different now, all of a sudden?

Because a woman named B.J. Gray had come into his life and made him so damned dissatisfied with himself that he ached with wanting to be more, to be better, to be different. Different how? Better than what? More what?

He left his studio, deep in thought, and was still pondering when he flopped into bed again and switched off the light. *More worthy.* The answer came just as he was about to slide into sleep and it brought him sitting erect with a muffled curse.

Worthy enough. He had never seen himself as unworthy before, except when he looked through the eyes of the Dutchman. Now was he to see himself that way again because one particular woman, who was surely becoming much too important, might see him that way?

He was on the verge of sleep again when a memory popped into his head. *This time.* What had she meant by that? She'd said, *Why should anything be different this time?* This time as opposed to what other time? But sleep came before he could start to sort that one out, and in the morning he forgot all about it in the bustle of breakfast with B.J. and the girls.

Was that disappointment he saw in her eyes when he shouldered his pack and prepared to go out for the day alone—or was it relief? He pondered it as he hiked, considered it as he sat patiently waiting for subjects to photograph or sketch, but was still no closer to an answer when he arrived home again just as dusk came.

Laura heard him while he was taking off his boots in the back entry. "Hi, Uncle Cal," she said, letting both swinging doors flop back and forth as she came into the kitchen from the lounge. "You were gone a long time today."

"Hi, punkin." He set his boots on the plastic mat and entered the kitchen himself. "I had a lot to do." And a lot to think about.

"Oh. Well, you missed a great dinner. We had chili and toast."

"Oh? That's nice," he said, wishing he'd hadn't felt compelled to stay away for the sake of his own sanity. The last chili he'd eaten had come from a can. He'd thought it was all right, but the girls had complained bitterly. He really should make an effort to learn to cook, he knew, but the only time he thought about it was when he was hungry, and then it was too late. He needed something already prepared. Like now. His stomach growled hungrily as he opened the refrigerator. Was there any of B.J.'s chili left? If there was, he was having it, regardless of whether she meant it for the girls' lunch the next day. Unless he could change her mind, she wouldn't even be there at lunchtime tomorrow and she'd never know and . . .

And there was no chili in the fridge.

"Want me to ask B.J. to fix you something, Uncle Cal?"

"No, I do not!" he said, slamming the refrigerator door and slapping a pound of sliced bacon onto the counter.

"Laura!" Kara called. "It's on."

"Oops. Time to go. B.J.'s letting us watch 'Jeopardy!' tonight. She says it's educational, but I think it's just because she likes it. She's so smart, Uncle Cal, that she nearly always gets the right answers. Questions, I mean."

"Good for her."

"You're sure grumpy, Uncle Cal."

"Sorry. I'm tired."

He cooked himself bacon and eggs, thinking of the cholesterol, wondering if she would feel guilty if he dropped dead from clogged arteries. He wasn't even sure if chili was more healthful than eggs, but he'd have preferred it anyway. Oh, hell! he thought. Why did she ever have to come there? Shoving his half-eaten meal aside, he rested his chin on his hands and smiled. He was glad she had come. Even if she'd turned him inside out, even if she meant to, leave tomorrow, he wasn't going to let her out of his life.

He went into his studio, not turning his head at the sound of the gameshow host's voice as he crossed the far side of the lounge. Yet the memory of her perfect profile followed him. How could that be, when he hadn't even looked at her, for heaven's sake? Memory. That was what. She was imprinted on his damn memory.

He picked up the sketchpad he'd filled last night before he'd finally slept, and looked at the faces drawn on each page. B.J. laughing. B.J. pensive. B.J., her mouth tremulous, her eyes filled with something he'd never be able to name as he drew a brush from her toes to her thigh. B.J., her eyes closed as they'd been when he'd lifted her unconscious body into his arms. B.J., her lips all puffy and damp from his kiss, and her eyes bewildered, with a whole lot of questions in them . . . and a hint of hunger. B.J., B.J., B.J., on every page.

Cal groaned and flipped the pad shut so he couldn't see the sketches. It didn't help. She was there, in the front of his mind, as she had been all day. In the back of his mind. In the middle of his mind. Maybe he should just go to bed, seek oblivion in sleep, but it was too early. Besides, he'd just lie there and think of her. He swallowed hard. Why was he having so much difficulty with this? Always before, when he spotted a lady to his liking, if she seemed the slightest bit willing or interested, he'd known exactly what to do, how to handle it. So what was the damned difference this time?

The fact that she was the most beautiful woman he'd ever seen didn't account for it. The fact that he went weak in the knees and soft in the head in her presence didn't account for it. No, there was something else, and he didn't know what it was. He wished he'd inherited his father's analytical mind, as his brother had. How would Curt handle something like this? He'd sort it out, step by step. Okay, so he'd try it.

One: He wanted B.J. Gray. Two: She probably

wanted him, too, but was determined to ignore the situation. Which led to the question: Why did he continue to want a woman who had made it clear that she wasn't going to give in to anything so basic as lust? Answer: Because some elusive quality of hers had skewed his normal reactions. But what, dammit? What?

Then, with a flash of insight, he knew: the lady might be interested, but she wasn't exactly willing.

And why not? Why should she be so unwilling to give him a chance? Why should she resist his every attempt at friendship? Why did she have to walk away just when things were starting to get stimulating between them? Did she think he couldn't see that enchanting little pulse in her throat, the one that went wild when he stroked his fingers down her cheek, or touched her foot, kissed her lips . . . or her toes?

He smiled pensively. Never in his life had he kissed a woman's toes before he had so much as kissed her breasts! She was driving him insane! She had bewitched him.

He groaned silently, flinging the sketchpad to a shelf. He was crazy to have wasted so much time and paper making sketches of her. He only made sketches preliminary to painting, and he did not paint portraits. Ergo, he should not be sketching B.J. Gray. And he would not do it again.

Seven

Cal closed up his paint tube, set his brush into its
solution, and ran his hands through his hair. He
couldn't concentrate. He couldn't even think. He
wanted . . . something.

In the kitchen, he lifted the lid of the deep freeze,
rummaging through it for a dessert of some kind.
The cook who spent all summer catering to the guests
must have left a pie or two, or a cake for him. And
right now he needed something. Something sweet.
Something substantial. Something he could get his
teeth into before he went storming through the rest
of the house searching for the sweetest morsel he
had seen or tasted in years.

One who had turned her back on him. Walked
away.

"Ah," he muttered. "Fruitcake." He unwrapped it.
"How appropriate."

It was frozen solid.

"Jeopardy!" was over and B.J. was playing a board
game with the girls when he slipped quietly into the

lounge and took a chair near them. Picking up a book from a nearby table, he held it open on his lap, his eyes downcast as if he were reading. He wasn't. He was listening.

" 'What would you do if you saw someone shoplifting?' " Kara asked, reading from a card. " 'Tell a clerk? Walk away and pretend you'd seen nothing? Quietly tell the shoplifter that you'd seen and give him or her a chance to put the item back?' "

B.J. groaned. "Why do I always get the real tough ones that can't be answered without qualification? If it was a young person who might be doing it on a dare or because he or she didn't really know better, I'd tell the shoplifter to put it back. But if it was an adult or an older teenager, I'd tell the manager. But what if it was a very poor person who was stealing to eat? Lord, kids, I don't know!"

"You have to give an answer," Kara said gleefully. "One of the above."

Out of the corner of his eye, Cal watched B.J. ponder the question, her chin on one fist. When she finally answered, he gave up all pretense of reading and listened openly as she said, "I'd have to tell the manager, regardless, because shoplifting is stealing and even if a person's hungry, there are other ways. But I wouldn't like it."

"Want to play, Uncle Cal?" Laura asked, seeing his interest.

"I . . . uh, don't know how." But he got to his feet, drawn to the table as if by the magnet of B.J.'s presence.

"Oh, it's easy. And fun. And you learn all sorts of things about your friends and family and even yourself," said his niece, pushing a chair away from the card table with one foot in further invitation. Cal took the chair and sat across from B.J. The girls explained in confusing detail how to play the game, but when they started again it began to make sense.

They all laughed as they learned that Kara most definitely would not tell a man his zipper was undone. She nearly hid under the table at the thought. Laura adamantly expressed her belief that using the wrong bus transfer was all right if the driver didn't notice. The bus company had more money than she did.

But it was B.J.'s responses to moral dilemmas that interested Cal. She seldom saw things as black or white, and agonized over her responses, trying to see every side before she made a decision. "It's not right to laugh at ethnic jokes," she said. "But—"

"B.J.! You're really bad at this game," Laura complained. "You can't have buts and ifs. You have to use the answers that are on the card." She read the card again. " 'You've always hated ethnic jokes, but your boss tells you a really mean, but hilariously funny one. You would laugh politely and quit your job? You would tell your boss you didn't like that kind of humor and ask him not to tell you any more ethnic jokes? You would laugh, in spite of your feelings, because the joke was really funny?' "

B.J. groaned and covered her face with one hand. "All right. I have to admit it. I'd laugh, if it was really funny. I know that. I've done it. But I'd feel bad for a long, long time and think a lot less of myself. Okay?"

"You still stuck a *but* in there," Laura said, writing down a number on a scorecard, "but at least you chose an answer."

As the game proceeded Cal was amazed at the things he discovered about himself as well. Like B.J., he couldn't view life with the black and white certainties children did. He found himself sharing wry smiles with her, understanding glances, the odd chuckle at the definite responses the girls made without any adult-type waffling.

"It's easy to be right when you're eleven," she murmured.

"It is. Almost as easy as when you're twenty-three."

She knew he was referring to his first encounter with the artist who was to become his mentor, and smiled gently. "We all grow up eventually."

Cal was sad when it was time for the girls to go to bed. He'd been enjoying the evening very much and didn't want it to end. With the kids tucked in and kissed good night by both their temporary guardians, and the light turned off in their room, he took B.J.'s hand as if it were the most natural thing in the world and walked down the corridor with her.

"I have a treat for us in the kitchen."

She lifted her brows. "Oh? What's that?"

"Something really, really special, and far too good for children, which is why I didn't tell them about it. That, and the fact that it was frozen solid and I forgot about it until they were safely in bed. Freud would say I'd done it deliberately."

B.J. had to laugh as she looked at the "treat" he had for her. She bit her lip and shook her head. "Not for me, thanks. I'm not hungry."

"Well, damn!" he said. He dragged a hand through his hair, leaving it standing up in little tufts that caught the overhead light and glistened blue black. Some instinctive, feminine part of her wanted to smooth it down. "After all the trouble I went to, opening the lid of the deep freeze, bending over, pulling the cake out and leaving it here to thaw, all that work—for nothing. Lady, you have wounded me grievously."

She laughed at his tale of drudgery, but he scowled severely at her and said, "Besides, I think you're lying." Holding up an imaginary card, pretending to read, he went on pontifically, " 'If somebody offers you food that you truly dislike, do you accept it and choke it down? Do you refuse politely by claiming not to be hungry? Do you tell the truth about the way you feel and hope they'll offer you something else?' No waffling. You must choose one of the above."

"And I did," she said. "I'm really not terribly hungry."

"Don't you ever eat something just because it might taste good, whether you're hungry or not?"

Her face went very still. "No," she said quietly.

He looked at her quizzically. "But do you like fruitcake when you are hungry?"

Again her eyes smiled. "Sadly for my waistline, yes."

He wanted to tell her there was nothing wrong with her waistline. "But even if you hated it, you'd never have chosen the third option, would you?"

"Why do you say that?"

"Because I think you're afraid of what I might have offered you in its place."

"I'm not so much afraid, Cal, as naturally cautious."

He nodded, and wanted with a sudden and shocking hunger to make that other offer, to pull her into his arms and kiss the living daylights out of her. He wanted to lift her up and carry her to his bed and make slow, sweet love to her whether she was emotionally ready or not.

His smile tilted one side of his mouth. "You're probably right to exercise caution."

"The girls have told me what an awful cook you are," she said with a laugh. "I understand your spaghetti sauce tastes like dog food."

He joined in her laughter. It was easy to laugh with her, he thought, taking pleasure in the fact. It was wonderful having someone to enjoy things with. Linking his fingers with hers again, he led her to the table and seated her ceremoniously. "I promise not to offer you anything I'm responsible for having cooked, and if you're really not hungry, will you at least pretend a bit of thirst?"

"No pretense necessary," she assured him.

He smiled and took a bottle of Riesling from the refrigerator, then poured it into two glasses, leaving the bottle on the table.

B.J. examined the label. "Thank goodness. I've heard stories about homemade wines and what they can do to the unwary."

He gave her a stern look. "You," he said, "do not qualify as 'unwary.' "

She shrugged and smiled, dropping her lashes, but she didn't deny it.

"B.J." He swallowed hard. "Lord, but you do things to me when you flirt like that."

She looked up, startled. "Like what? I don't flirt!"

He whispered a fingertip across the back of her hand. "Oh, yes, you do, lady, and every time you bat those long lashes at me and give me tantalizing little glimpses of those big blue eyes, I get all hot and bothered and ready to—roar. You just don't know how pretty you are."

Her eyes flared wider for a second before her lashes fluttered in confusion. "Cal . . . don't," she said, then looked down in that way he was beginning to suspect meant that she was moved and didn't want to show it.

"Okay," he said. "But I don't know why you don't like compliments. Especially sincere ones."

She smiled at him briefly before those incredible lashes flickered down again, and he shook his head as it dawned on him that she wasn't flirting. She *didn't* have the faintest idea of how it affected him when she caught him in the quick web of her gaze, then looked down like that. In any other woman of his acquaintance, that mannerism would have been a carefully contrived one, likely practiced for hours in front of a mirror. With B.J., though, it was completely unconscious. It endeared her to him even more and he felt a hard, hot lump rise up in his throat. She was so damned special, and she didn't have a clue.

"Look at me," he whispered.

Startled, B.J. glanced up at him, finding the air suddenly crackling with electricity. Her eyes widened as he drew one thumb across her lower lip.

"It's happening again," he said.

"What is?"

"I keep getting this overwhelming urge to kiss you."

Her heart hammered in her chest. "I don't think it's a really great idea."

He could see the wild little pulse in her throat. In a minute he was going to press his mouth to that pulse. The anticipation made him harden and ache. "Don't you?"

She shook her head.

"Why not? Give me three good reasons."

She smiled. That she could do. "I don't know you very well and I don't make a habit of kissing strangers, recent examples notwithstanding. And I'm leaving tomorrow."

"I could say that those were only two reasons, but I'll be kind. I wish you wouldn't go so soon." Again he smoothed his thumb over her lower lip, just to watch its unconscious pout. "Couldn't someone else look in on your friend's house? I have a radiophone here. You could call someone."

"No. I have to leave." She twisted her head to one side, and his hand fell to the table between them. "But not just because of my commitments there, Cal," she said, looking down at his hand, touching it with the tips of her fingers. She shuddered, thinking of the way his caresses made her feel. It was a feeling she liked. A feeling she wanted. *A feeling?* No. A whole series of them, each one more potent than the other, exploding in little pops of excitement all through her blood.

"Because of something I've said or done?" he asked.

"It's not just you," she said quietly, then paused, nibbling at her lower lip. "Suddenly things are happening that I never thought would happen to me, and they're happening awfully fast." She remembered too well how fast things had happened with Kevin, the man at Club Caribbean, and then, her involvement hadn't been nearly as emotional. This time she knew she was falling in love. Before she had merely, as Melody put it, been falling in lust. A perfectly normal process, Mel had insisted, but one B.J. had felt compelled to halt. While she had wanted Kevin, she hadn't really liked him. Trouble was, she liked Cal . . . along with loving him.

"Sometimes," Cal said gently, "we can't help how fast things happen. I wish it didn't worry you so much."

"But it does. There doesn't seem to be a proper background for any of this, no solid fabric behind it." And she still hadn't told him the truth about herself. "We seem to have missed out a few steps, Cal. It's like knitting. If you miss stitches, the garment is in danger of falling apart later on." She smiled, and her dimples flickered so quickly he nearly missed them, but the expression in her eyes stopped his heart.

And he was in danger of falling in love with her, he thought, then blinked rapidly, wondering where that idea had sprung from. He crushed it down. He wouldn't even consider it. He wanted her, sure, but anything else was out of the question. Preposterous. Like she said, they'd known each other for three and a half days, and if things were happening too fast for her, they were right on schedule for him. He had only to remember that moving fast was the best way to allay doubts and apprehensions. If they connected before either of them had too much time to think, there'd be no turning back and this entire episode could go on until its natural end. Then he would be able to start forgetting about her.

"Maybe we've missed out a few stitches or steps," he said softly, thoughtfully, "but neither of us is a child, B.J., and you're becoming more and more important to me each moment we spend together. No, don't shake your head. I have to tell you this.

"I've never felt quite like this about another woman." That much, he knew, was true, and he didn't mind admitting it. "I've never before known anybody with such—innate honesty. It makes me want to be totally honest with you." He frowned. Was that true? After a moment's reflection, he decided, yes, it was.

B.J. cringed inside. How had he come to develop such a false opinion of her? She had to tell him! But how? How to begin? She'd tried to make him see reality last night, but he hadn't listened. He had just said again that she was beautiful. And while it was nice to hear—no, more than nice, it was wonderful and made her feel all mushy and hot inside—it was also too fantastic to believe. Her mirror said "pretty," other people agreed, and when she compared herself with what she had been before, she rejoiced inwardly. But beautiful? The word made her uncomfortable for reasons she couldn't begin to understand. "I'm just an ordinary woman, Cal. I'm—"

"Hush." He smoothed his fingers over her lips, and she hushed, more because the delight coursing through her made it impossible for her to catch her breath than because he had told her not to speak. "I want to say this. I tried last night, but I couldn't find the right words and then you ran away. There's nothing ordinary about you at all, B.J. In spite of your beauty, there's an openness about you that so many other women seem to lack with their fakery, their games, their pretending to like a man so they can get from him whatever they want. I don't think you ever do that, do you, B.J.?"

Openness? She jerked her head back. "Cal, please. I . . . have to tell you something about myself. I'm—"

"That's what I mean," he interrupted, watching the color come and go in her face. "You're embarrassed by my saying this, and that's because you're so unassuming, so natural. If you like someone, it's because they've earned that liking. And if you don't, you'd never pretend, even if playing the game meant getting something you want. You didn't feign liking for me, even though you wanted to be here with the kids and I was standing in your way. You didn't try to charm me into letting you stay." He chuckled. "But in spite of that, you did charm me, and I want you to stay."

"But I don't want to stay," she lied desperately, hoping to convince herself, too. "I can't!"

She grabbed up her glass and drank deeply, hoping she wouldn't choke, then set it down because her hand was trembling too much for her to hold on to it.

"I'm upsetting you, I know," he said quietly. "Maybe even scaring you, but please, don't be afraid. Drink some more wine, B.J. You're too pale." He lifted her glass to her lips, feeding her the wine, and she drank, her eyes on his. No one had ever done something like this to her before and she didn't know how to tell him to stop, or even if she wanted to tell him that.

"Your complexion," he said, setting her glass down and stroking her cheek. "That was something I noticed about you immediately. There you were, white as a sheet, yet your skin was still like porcelain, clear and flawless. Other people pay vast sums to cosmetic companies to achieve what you have naturally. And your hair was like spun silk, the scent of you as clean and as fresh as a new morning, and it was all real. You hadn't achieved that look by artifice. No chemicals, no makeup, no hiding behind something synthetic. There's an honesty about you that shines forth and . . ."

And what? he asked himself, feeling something rise in him like a great, hard lump of need that grew and grew. It was such a huge need, so vast and overwhelming that he thought he might pass out as his head spun and his chest ached. He struggled for breath, fought to understand what was happening to him, and felt it burst free with such a force, he nearly cried out in pain. But it was there, the pain was gone, leaving behind such an exhilaration, such an excitement, such a sense of utter fulfillment, for just a second he thought he understood how a woman must feel at the moment of birth.

"B.J.! Oh, B.J., I want to paint you," he said in a hushed but exultant tone. "Yes! That's it! I have to!" Now, the reason for the sketches became clear. Some secret part of him had known all along that this was his destiny. B.J. In oils.

She sat back, staring at him, feeling as utterly dumbfounded as he looked. No! He hadn't said those words! Had he?

"Cal? Do you know what you just said?"

"Yes!" he exclaimed, laughing excitedly. "I don't know where the idea came from, but I know it's right. It's what has to be." He lifted his glass and drained it, then recklessly refilled it.

Of course! That was what his tortured thoughts had all been about the night before. He wanted to paint her. To do that, he had to be worthy not only as a painter, but as a man, and he didn't know if he was. Because in order to paint her, he was going to have to know her—totally—and she would have to know him, trust him, give him every nuance of herself, even the small things she might now be holding back.

He caught both her hands in his, gripped them tightly. "Let me do it, B.J. Let me paint you."

"You don't paint portraits."

Her voice was hoarse with the fear that rushed over her. She drew in a sharp breath and felt herself flushing as his earlier words echoed in her mind. Purity of soul? No artifice? If he only knew! If he tried to paint her, if he looked that closely, he would see the sham just under the veneer of what he called "purity." He was an artist known for his ability to discover the essence of the creatures he painted. Realism was his trademark. He could capture the primitive emotions of animals—the burning fury of a dam whose young were threatened; the spirit of a predator spying its prey; the wary alertness of a doe at a watering hole; the arrogance of a sea lion bellowing out his intentions to the world.

If he painted her, he would have to look too closely. Surely he'd see beneath the carapace of her deception, discover the counterfeit that she really was. And did she want him to know the truth? Did she want to change that beautiful—if totally false—impression he had of her? *No!* something in her wailed. She liked having him see her as he did.

"You can't paint me," she said. "You can't. If you want to do portraits, do them. I have faith in you. You can paint them if you choose to, but not me."

"I can. I will." His grip on her hands was almost painful. His eyes were black with the passion of his dream. "But only if it's you. I can be what I want, finally, thanks to you. Don't deny me this, B.J. It's my dream, and you can make it come true. No one else. Just you. I have to try."

How could she deny him his dream? Yet how could she let him discover the truth about her? He would hate her if he did, and suddenly she knew she couldn't bear it if he hated her.

"No, Cal," she whispered. "Please, no."

"Why not?" He relaxed his grip and caressed instead, trying to wipe away the white marks his fingers had left on the back of her hand. His gaze held hers, intent, insistent. "Sweetheart, don't be afraid. I only want to paint you."

Only? He heard himself say the word and knew what a terrible misrepresentation it was. The painting would be only a small part of the bond he would require with her.

"B.J., please. Why not?" he asked, reading the inflexible denial in her eyes.

"Because." She trembled and withdrew her hands from his, as if he could read the truth simply through touching her. "Because we don't really know each other and . . . I think we'd have to."

"Yes." He stared at her, wondering if she understood as much as he thought she did, as much as he was just now beginning to understand himself. He knew with an unprecedented depth of self-knowledge that if he didn't try to paint her, he would be forever dissatisfied with his growth not only as an artist, but as a man. Looking at her, he realized he was hovering on the brink of a huge step. If he took it, he might falter. But if he didn't, he would simply shrivel up where he sat.

"Yes, B.J., we'll have to know each other very well." Know her? He was going to have to love her. The realization rose slowly within him, and he reeled as if from a powerful blow. Not just make love to her. *Love her.*

He stared at her. Did he? Had it really happened to him at last? And suddenly he knew it had. He wasn't just "in danger" of falling in love with B.J. Gray. He'd up and done it! He wanted to laugh at himself at the same time as he wanted to curse and deny it. Yet there was no denying it. It was so clear now, so obvious, and it explained all his nebulous feelings of the past few days.

Cal smiled at her, and the gentle tenderness in that smile stirred something inside B.J. that had slept for too long. She hushed it as best she could, and tried not hear the seduction in his voice as he said, "It won't happen right away, B.J., but it will happen."

"What will?" Her voice cracked.

"We'll know each other . . . well enough." His smile faded. He reached out and touched the back of her hand again.

She smiled faintly and looked down. "Could we? Ever?"

"Couldn't we?" he countered. She felt more than saw his dark gaze on her, and her rapid pulse slowed to a heavy, almost lethargic beat that pounded in every recess and extremity of her body. "B.J.?"

"Yes?" she whispered, her fingers tight around the stem of her glass as she fought to withstand the pressures of that steady, deep cadence in her blood. She lifted her lashes and looked at him.

"Do you want . . . to know me that well?" he asked.

"Cal, stop it. I don't want this kind of—flirtation."

His eyes flared for a moment, with desire, she thought, but also with anger, with confusion. Only . . . what did he have to be confused about? He was in control of things here, wasn't he? In control not only of his own emotions, but of hers. She was the one hanging on by the tips of her nails, about to fall over the cliff.

"Why would it have to be a flirtation?" he asked. "Don't you think I'm capable of anything else?"

She frowned at the pain in his tone. This wasn't the way it was supposed to be. This was Cal Mixall, womanizer-at-large. Was this some kind of act? If it were, it was a damned good one, she thought, but brought herself up short. "Frankly, no."

"Well, I am!" *I love you!* he wanted to tell her, but it was still too new, too unbelievable even to him. Could a man really fall in love in so short a time? Of course he could. He had, but if it was too soon for him to fully comprehend it, how could he expect her to believe it? He would have to show her. The thought of showing her how much he cared for her made him tremble deep inside.

"How do you know you are?" she asked. "You've never tried anything else."

"What makes you so sure?"

B.J. had no answer. Really, she had no reason to believe he was the philanderer she'd always thought him to be. Just the odd comment made by Curtis, or one of the amusing stories passed on by Melody, possibly embellished to add interest. After all, it was only in the past two years that Cal had even been on this side of the country and in frequent contact with his brother and sister-in-law. What he'd done, the kind of life he'd led, back east was a mystery to her. And in truth, so was his life since he'd come to the coast, though they might live only ten or fifteen miles apart. More than distance separated them. They had different life-styles, different circles of friends. As for the few snippets that had appeared in the arts and literature pages of the papers, gossip didn't count. She'd never listened to it about other people; why was she so ready to believe the worst of Cal?

She looked up and found him waiting. "I'm sorry," she said. "That was an unfair comment on my part. I don't know what you might or might not have tried and it's none of my business."

"It has recently become your business," he said huskily, touching her face gently with one fingertip, then two, then four, stroking them from her temple to her chin. "I want you to like me. I want us to know each other. Explore each other's . . . feelings."

All her physical senses urged her to lean against his hand, while all her mental capacities shrieked at her to get up, to leave, to run as far and as fast as she could. Loving this man could mean her destruction. But it was too late to run. She drew in a tremulous breath and let it out slowly. And leaned.

"Cal, when you touch me, I can't think."

His smile tore her heart to pieces. "You're too honest, my beautiful B.J. You shouldn't have said that, because now I'm not going to let you think. I'm only going to make you feel."

He slid his fingers to her ear, traced the outline of it with just one, then moved and pressed softly against that mad little pulse in her throat. He watched her eyes flare with shining violet lights before she lowered her lids. But she didn't pull away from him.

"What do you feel when I touch you like that?"

She swallowed. He saw her throat work convulsively. She lifted her lids, those thick, dark lashes fluttering up until she met his gaze. "Warm. Tingly."

"Good," he said softly. "Because when I touch you, I feel hot. And throbbing."

She remembered their kisses. That was the way they had made her feel, too, hot and throbbing. She wanted those feeling again now even though she was still afraid. She wished she wasn't afraid, wished she had the experience she knew she needed in order to meet this man on even ground, play the game his way. Because if she wanted him—and she did—she'd have to play by his rules. They were the only ones available. She didn't have any of her own.

He'd asked her if she wanted to know him *that well*. Did she? All the new and tremulous love inside her whispered that she did, and she listened to it while she gazed into his eyes. She wasn't kidding herself. She knew what would have to happen before they knew each other with the depth necessary to accomplish what he wanted. That it wasn't so with all artists and their subjects, she also knew. But he wasn't any other artist. And she wasn't any other subject. And there was something between them that precluded ordinary reactions, ordinary treatment of his desire to paint her. His desire—and hers—went so far beyond that, that the painting, if it ever materialized, would simply be another way of expressing emotion growing too deep for words.

But was it that deep on both their sides? Could she trust him as much as she knew she'd have to? No! Not yet. She knew she couldn't, because it would mean telling him the truth about herself and she wasn't ready to do that yet. If only, she thought, fighting the desire to run again, if only he'd never told her he found her beautiful.

"Cal," she said pleadingly, "don't ask that of me. Ask anything else, but not to paint me."

His right hand slid around to cup the back of her head. "Anything?" he asked lazily, combing his fingers through her hair. "This?"

"What?" She could scarcely think, let alone speak coherently.

"This," he said again, and it was no longer a question. He urged her head forward, pulling her toward him.

Then he kissed her.

It was nothing like any other kiss they had shared. It was nothing like anything she had ever experienced. This was a kiss from him that said, *Here I am, take me,* to which she answered fervently, *Me too.* In that moment she knew she was lost.

The corner of the table prevented their bodies from touching, but somehow that wasn't important. His mouth was firm on hers, demanding, and his skin smelled wonderful, of after-shave or cologne, of the soap from his shower, the shampoo in his hair, and that faint, elusive scent that she couldn't place. The tip of her tongue tasted his lower lip, once, twice, then a third time, and she finally realized what that scent, that taste, was. It made it exclusively his.

She withdrew her mouth from his, laughing delightedly, burying her face in the crook of his neck, drawing in the scent that matched the taste.

"Joke?" he asked in a wobbly tone. Pressing her head to him, he reveled in her scent, the texture of her hair, her willingness to come close to him.

"You taste like turpentine."

His hand cradled the nape of her neck, fingers tangling to her hair, tugging gently. He wanted to see her face. "I'm sorry."

"No," she said, her dimples dancing in her cheeks. "I love the taste of turpentine. Now."

His eyes flared with something that both elated and terrified her. "B.J?" he gasped, but she couldn't let him go on. Clasping his head between her hands, she pulled his mouth back to hers. He met her kiss with a soft groan of capitulation, his mouth opening over hers, hard and insistent. Love, strong and special, began to grow inside her where no such thing had ever lived before.

Eight

It was a warmth, to begin with, then a heat. It expanded, intensifying, until she thought she might melt and fall to the floor. She didn't because of the firmness of his lips on hers, and the hard hand between her shoulder blades, the other supporting her head. He parted her mouth with the force of his lips, and his tongue slid over her teeth, between them, lapping at hers, tangling with it, and she returned its caresses ardently, avidly, until her head spun with lack of air. But who needed to breathe at a time like this? she wondered, then quit wondering, quit thinking, and simply felt.

But as if he, too, were suffering from the same lack of oxygen, he lifted his head, gasping. His eyes blazed into hers with undeniable joy as they both breathed hard, then they came together again as if compelled.

His hand tightened, slipped down to her nape and then to her waist as he deepened the kiss, his tongue plunging into her mouth with a hard, sensual rhythm that set up a reciprocal beat in her blood, in her body, in her female core. She met it with her tongue, returning it measure for measure, until he growled and tore his mouth from hers. She caught his head with both hands again, not wanting him to leave, but he had no such intention anyway. His burning lips pressed to her throat, and his tongue covered the pulse she could feel pounding there. He drew on it, sucking gently, then harder, and she knew what would happen if he continued. Did she want his mark on her? Yes, yes, yes! If he wanted to put that kind of mark on her, then that was what she wanted, too. She was way, way out of her depth, but she also realized that even if she didn't know how to swim in these waters, maybe drowning wasn't such a bad way to go.

Cal heard her make a small sound that might have been protest and he responded to it at once, easing up with little lip-nips against her mouth and cheeks and chin, until she sighed and sank back in her chair. Her hands trailed from his hair to his shoulders and then away, breaking the contact completely.

She stared at the tabletop.

"Sorry," he said finally, his breathing ragged. "That kind of got out of hand."

"Yes." It was all she could do to whisper her agreement. He picked up her hand. His was shaking and he made no attempt to hide that from her.

She drew in several more breaths, then said, "Cal?" lifting to him eyes almost violet with passion.

"Yes, love?"

"Do you have any idea what a patookus is?"

"What?" His sputter of laughter was a necessary release of tension. "Not the faintest. Why?"

"Oh . . . nothing. Just something Melody said."

His smile was rueful. "Oh, that Melody. She set us up, you know."

Again she gave him that startled-doe look. "I know. I didn't realize you did. I'm sorry, Cal. I shouldn't have come under the circumstances."

He shook his head in denial of her words. The circumstances being that he was crazy in love for the first time in his life. It was all he could do to calm himself enough to say, "But you did come, and I wouldn't have it any other way, B.J. Melody may be an interfering nuisance, but I intend to thank her with all appropriate profusion for sending you to me."

Alarm filled her eyes. Now that he was no longer kissing her, touching her, she could think more clearly. "I'm still leaving, of course. I don't . . . have casual affairs, Cal."

He sighed inwardly. He'd known all along it was too soon for her. She wasn't running this race at the same pace as he was if she was still thinking along the lines of casual affairs. But he'd wait for her. If it took forever, he'd wait.

"Of course," he said. "I know that. But you don't have to leave as soon as you'd planned, B.J. Please? Not right away?" Hell, he might be willing to wait, but was there anything wrong with trying to encourage her to catch up?

She looked at him as she got to her feet, and he hated the way her eyes were big and scared. Never had he less wanted a woman to walk away from him, though that she was ready to do so was, in itself, unique. Was there anything about B.J. Gray that wasn't?

At the door she turned back. "I have to," she said jerkily. "Monday." Her eyes widened as she realized just how soon that was. Tomorrow! She didn't want to leave tomorrow, or any other day soon, but she knew she had to. Anything else would be insane.

He nodded, swallowing his disappointment. He wouldn't push. "Of course," he said again. "But you'll be back."

He watched her breasts rise as she drew in a deep breath. "I don't think so."

"Yes, you will," he said, but he let her go because he knew if he kept her there, held her again, touched her in any way, he'd be unable to stop himself this time.

The girls' tears when she left the next morning made B.J. feel like a monster, but she could comfort them with the promise that she'd see them again in only two weeks. In two weeks Cal would fly out to get her. Two weeks? If it seemed long to the girls, it was an eternity to her.

She turned to Cal, wondering how to say good-bye. She didn't want to spend two weeks away from him. She wanted to crawl into the haven of his arms and rest her head on his chest. She wanted to spend long nights hearing his heart beat under her ear, feeling his breath on her cheek, learning how to please him and how to take the enormous pleasure she was just beginning to think she was capable of feeling. She wanted to do anything but leave, only . . . she had to. She knew that. She wasn't ready for him, not the way he wanted her to be. The only way for either of them to stand it, was for her to leave and do her thinking, her growing up—if that was what was needed—out of his sight.

She met his dark gaze for a moment, then said, "See you soon." He nodded. Pulling her helmet on, she straddled the bike, started the engine, and gunned it. Flying up the hill, she stuck to the trail this time, avoiding the now-dried mud at the side of the irrigation ditch.

She didn't stop and look back until she was high above the valley. When she did, there was no one to see, no one to wave to, no one watching her disappear into the thickness of the forest. She waved anyway, and drove on.

After the ferry trip across the mouth of Jervis

Inlet, she whipped along the Sunshine Coast high-way, a twisted, convoluted torture track for drivers of four-wheeled vehicles, but a delight for her. She made such good time, she had to wait for the ferry to take her across Howe Sound. She sat by the window in the passenger lounge once the ship had sailed, gazing at the tall, jagged mountains, think-ing of a secluded valley that lay beyond them, and ached as she longed for the sound of Cal's voice, the touch of his hand, and the scent of his skin. How could he have become so important to her in only a few days? She couldn't believe how much she missed him.

As the days passed she missed him even more.

What was Cal doing right now? she wondered, walking the seawall in Stanley Park on Tuesday af-ternoon while a light drizzle fell. Wednesday, at dusk, as she drew the curtains in the house she was tak-ing care of, she wondered if he was safely back home from wherever he'd gone that day. What awful con-coction would he make for dinner? she mused, smil-ing. Was it something the kids would eat willingly, or would he have to suffer through their "whining and dining"? Would they think it looked or tasted like dog food?

She wondered idly how they knew what dog food tasted like, but she knew that at least they wouldn't be existing on peanut butter sandwiches and canned tomato soup, not with what she'd left in the freezer. Did he know about those meals? she asked herself on Thursday evening as she sat curled up with a book whose pages she would have to read again. Had the kids told him about the leftover chili, the leftover stew? The tuna casseroles and the lasagne? Had he been eating them, too, and thinking of her?

She was still wrapped up in thinking about him on Friday afternoon when she drove her car into the garage at the rear of her friend's house. Entering through the kitchen, she glanced at the small chicken breast thawing in the sink and turned away. She wasn't hungry. Not for that. She didn't know what she wanted. She kicked off her shoes, hung her jacket in a closet, and padded across thick carpets into the living room, flicking on lights as she went. When the doorbell rang and she looked out the peephole, she thought she must have conjured him up through the power of her imagination, her need. But when she wrenched open the door and reached out to touch him, he was real, and solid, and soaking wet.

"Cal!" she cried. "What are you doing here?"

He answered her by hauling her against him and kissing her until she moaned, wrapped her arms around his waist, and clung to him.

"Glad to see me?" he asked when he came up for air.

She nodded, burying her face in the crook of his neck, breathing in the fresh scent of his skin, the tang that was exclusively his. But . . .

"No turpentine!" she murmured, lifting her head to look at him. "You haven't been working?"

"No," he said. "I couldn't. I missed you too much."

She forgot they hadn't known each other long enough. She forgot she wanted time to think about things. She forgot everything but the past empty days. "Oh, Cal, I missed you, too."

"Tell me," he said. "Tell me how much you've missed me."

Trembling, she lifted her hand and touched his face, smiling. "More than I should have, I think. But . . . what *are* you doing here? Where are the kids?" she added as an afterthought. Wow! Some coguardian she was! The girls should have been her first concern.

"Laura and Kara are at my place, safe and sound and happy. And as for me, I'm here because I couldn't stay away. By Monday afternoon I was pacing. By

Tuesday I couldn't eat. Wednesday night I didn't sleep. Thursday I asked the kids how they felt about moving back to town and their cheers nearly knocked me dead, and not only because of my weakened condition. So I'm here. And I have to kiss you again."

He did, and she knew why she had missed him.

"B.J.," he said several magic minutes later. "We have to stop this. We have to talk."

"Hmm?" she asked dreamily, tracing the shape of his mouth with one finger. One shaking finger, she noticed dimly. "Talk? I'd rather do this."

"Me too, but kisses aren't enough. I think maybe I'm going to have to make love to you."

"Really?" She sounded startled and he wanted to laugh.

"Really. So if you don't want me to do it out here in the rain—and in full view of the neighbors—invite me in"

"Neighbors?" What was he talking about?

"Yes. You know, the people across the street. Or next door. Or down the block. Any of them."

"Oh." Did he mean it? If she invited him in, would he make love to her?

"B.J. I'm getting wetter."

"Oh. Yes. Me too." She frowned in perplexity. What was making them wet? She couldn't concentrate while her mind was so filled with the possibilities that lay just around the corner, and her body was pounding with need.

He laughed, then scooped her off her feet and stepped inside. Shutting the door, he leaned on it and let her slide slowly down his front.

The laughter in his eyes died and he gazed at her seriously. "I had to come. I couldn't stand staying away from you. I know you're not ready yet, so I'm going to take it slow, make it easy on you, the way it should be. You'll get to know me, and then we'll decide where to go from there."

"Cal . . ." She wanted to tell him he was wrong. She wanted him to be wrong. But he wasn't. He was right, and she felt like a fool because of it. She swallowed the hard lump in her throat. "When did you arrive?"

"Around noon. I phoned you. Several times. I was going to ask you for a date. Dinner, dancing, the works. I was going to arrive with chocolates and wine and flowers. Instead, I came empty-handed. I got worried when I couldn't reach you by phone. I've been sitting on your doorstep in the drizzle for forty-five minutes, waiting for you to come home."

"How did you know I was home? Why didn't you wait in your car?"

"I had to park three blocks away thanks to that open house down the street. I rang the bell when I saw the lights come on. Where did you park?"

"The garage is reached through the back lane." Up on her tiptoes, she kissed him shyly. "I'm glad you didn't wait," she murmured. "I don't think I could have waited another week to see you. Let me go, Cal, and I'll get packed. I don't need dinner and dancing and flowers, and I never eat chocolate. Is there still enough daylight for us to make it back to the lake this evening?"

He stepped away from her and shrugged out of his wet jacket, hanging it on the brass coat stand by the door. "You didn't hear what I said, did you? I didn't come to take you back up to the lake for the weekend. I've changed my plans. I've moved the kids into my house and we'll stay there until their school reopens."

Her eyes widened. "But—"

He shut her mouth with one finger, lips curved into a satisfied smile, dark eyes soft and glowing. "But nothing. I need to be near you. The kids think it's a great idea. They've got a million plans just for the weekend. Dinner at McDonald's tonight with every friend they could reach this afternoon by phone, to catch up on all the latest kid gossip. They've been out of touch for nearly three weeks, an eternity to them. My treat, I told them. I'm buying their loyalty, to say nothing of their absence, so I can have a private dinner with you."

"But Cal—"

He interrupted her again. "It's all right. Everything's going to work out fine. I'm going to enroll them in a school near my place on Monday morning. I've already talked to the principal and the head of the school board, who both know that as soon as St. Agnes School is rebuilt, they'll be transferring back over here. They're in agreement."

She gaped. "You can't do that! Melody and Curt—"

"Won't mind," he finished for her. "When the school burned down and it was decided the girls would stay with me, they—and their parents—wanted it to be here in town, but I insisted it had to be at the lake so I could work."

"Yes," she said, wrapping her arms around herself. "You had to be at the lake so you could paint. I know. Melody told me. Cal, you have to work. Your exhibit in December . . ."

"I can't work." He took her hand and led her toward the living room he could see through an archway, with big squashy white sofas, lots of green plants, and a blue cockatoo in a brass cage. Tilting her face up to his, he said, "I've tried, B.J. I've tried to work since Monday afternoon. I want to paint, but the only thing I want to paint is you."

Her flush paled out to nothing. She looked down, but not before he saw misery dull the shine in her eyes. "No . . . I told you, Cal. No."

Turning her face to his, he smiled. "We'll see. Don't discount the idea completely, B.J. You might change your mind."

She knew she wouldn't. What she didn't know

was when she would find the courage to tell him about herself so that he would understand why she didn't want him to paint her. She frowned, gnawing on her lower lip. If he knew the truth, would he still want to paint her? Would he still . . . want her?

"Don't frown like that." He touched the grooves between her brows. "Oh, but I've missed being able to look at you, to touch you." His knuckles stroked over her cheek. She shivered at the delicate sensations his touch sent through her system. "No, don't tremble. I'm not going to hurt you," he said, but she slipped away from him, going to the window to look out over the rainy street.

She heard him sigh. "When does your friend—the one who owns this place—come back?"

She turned. "In a couple of weeks."

"And your plans then?"

His eyes, though hooded, were watching her intently, and she thought she knew the direction his thoughts were taking. "I don't have any, but by then Curt and Melody's house should have a clear corner in it somewhere for me. That's where I was all day. The renovations are coming along fine. You won't recognize the place, Cal. You'll remember it—if you recall it at all—as a gloomy Edwardian house with little windows and dark paneling. Well, when we're finished with it, it'll be bright and modern and beautiful, and even before it's done, I'll be more than comfortable there and—"

"Stop it," he said, crossing swiftly to her. "It's all right. I wasn't going to ask you to move in with me," he said with something less than absolute truth. He maybe hadn't been going to ask her right away, but in a couple of weeks things might be different.

"Oh." She didn't know whether to laugh or get mad. He was the first mind reader she'd ever known. "I didn't say you were."

"No, but you were afraid I was."

All right, she admitted to herself, maybe that was so. She'd been babbling like an idiot, panicked at the thought of his asking her to move into his house. She wondered what she was more afraid of, Cal, or the depths of her own burgeoning emotions.

But what would happen right now if, while she was so tense and agitated, he were to reach out and pull her into his arms? Would her tension explode into passion? Her body tautened, just thinking about it. She knew the longing she felt was only a portion of what she could feel. There was more, so much more, and she wanted it. Oh, Lord, how she wanted it! But . . .

He touched her shoulder. "It's okay," he said soothingly when she went rigid. "I'm not going to do anything you don't want me to do."

She drew in several calming breaths. "I know." She looked up at him, then turned to the window to draw the drapes against the coming dusk. Skirting him carefully, she walked to the other window and drew those drapes, enclosing Cal and herself in a cocoon of soft lamplight. Behind her, even though half the room separated them, she felt his closeness, his warmth, his magnetism. Deliciously so. Dangerously so, she thought, facing him. But it was the kind of danger that exhilarated and thrilled, like just before the big drop on a roller-coaster ride. She wanted to hold on to that sensation, even though she told herself she should go and change out of her damp cotton jumpsuit.

But while standing there in the warmly lighted room and looking at Cal might be dangerous, it was also too strong a temptation to withstand. A lamp cast a glow on his face that highlighted planes and angles she hadn't seen before. She moistened her lips, seeing that the sleeves of his yellow sweatshirt were pushed back, revealing strong wrists and forearms liberally covered with dark curling hair.

"B.J.," he said softly, "don't do that."

"Do what?"

"Look at me like that." Holding out a hand, he silently called her to him, and she went, unable to prevent herself.

She wanted to touch his arms, to experience the corded hard muscles she could see flexing as he clenched his fists at his side. She wanted to feel that hair under her palms. It reminded her of the narrow strip that ran down the center of his chest. Would it be as soft, or more wiry? It was certainly more luxuriant. Would it be echoed on his legs? His belly? She licked her dry lips again, and the touch of her tongue reminded her of the feel of his.

She ached to feel his mouth hot and hard and insistent on hers, chasing away all her doubts. Why couldn't she be like any other adult woman and go to the man she wanted, tell him she wanted him? He had said, jokingly, that he would make love to her outside if she didn't invite him in, yet when they had come into the house, he had hastened to assure her he had no intention of doing anything like that. Yet. And she was glad to let it ride, wasn't she? No matter how much she yearned for his touch, his voice murmuring love words in her ear, his breath warm and moist on her skin, his hands firm and loving on her body, she was still filled with a thousand doubts and a world of dread. . . .

"Could we sit down?" he asked.

"Yes, yes, of course. I'm sorry. Would you like a drink?"

He shook his head and took her hand, drawing her down with him onto a love seat. Curling an arm around her, he pulled her head onto his shoulder. "I just want to hold you for a few minutes before we go, to hear your voice, smell your hair. And maybe, in a little while, it will be safe for me to kiss you again." His arms tightened for a moment, then he sat forward, releasing her, half turning to look at her. "You said you were at Melody and Curt's all day. What do you do, supervise? And what kind of renovations are being done?"

"I don't supervise as much as get in the way, I suppose," she said. "But the architect and I think it's just as well for me to be on hand in case there's a question, even though she has it all laid out for the contractors. When it comes to knocking out walls and putting in skylights, nobody wants any mistakes to be made."

"That's how they go about making a gloomy Edwardian house less so?"

"That, and lowering ceilings, enlarging windows, and renovating the kitchen entirely. They're doing the upstairs now, so my room should be ready by the time the owner of this house comes back. And if it's not, there's bound to be one little corner somewhere free enough of plaster dust for me to camp out at home somewhere."

"Your room?" Cal raised his brows. "Home?"

"Of course. Oh, yes, you've heard us refer to it as Curt and Melody's house. It is, but it's my home, too. I grew up in that house, you know. As a matter of fact, I own it."

"Oh," he said blankly, then laughed at himself. "For some reason, I've thought of you as not having a home. I guess because you live at the school."

"Poor little waif with nowhere to go?" she said with an amused smile. "Just because I don't live there all the time doesn't make it less my home. When my parents died, since I was the only minor child, the house went to me, in trust. Mel and Curt rent from me, but I keep a room for myself—the same one I had as a child. I use it on weekends and during vacations from school."

"Why didn't Melody and Curt simply ask you to move in with the girls while they're away?"

"First, because I have a commitment at the school, although I don't absolutely have to live in, and second, because of the renovations. Besides, the girls wanted to board for a couple of terms. They've been day students and I think they're a bit envious of the boarders." She grinned. "I don't think that will last, once they've tried it."

"If they really hate it, they can always come back to me," he said, then added slyly, "And if you hate it, you could do the same."

"Cal, I've lived in that school for three years. I think if I were going to hate it, I'd have done so before now."

"Ah," he said, "but before now, you didn't know what you were missing." Bending his head, he closed his lips over hers, showing her what she'd be missing when she lived again in the school.

Her breathing was unsteady when she finally pushed him away. "I . . . get time off, you know."

His laughter warmed her. "Good. You're going to need it. But right now, I need a time out. Let's go see the girls before dinner."

Laura and Kara were ecstatic with the new plans, as Cal had said, and B.J. could see no reason to object —except the obvious one. Cal didn't like to work there and he had a show coming up in time to capture the Christmas trade.

"I can work here if I have to," he said. "Maybe seeing you every day will inspire me, and if it doesn't, I have quite a bit of work already done."

He showed her his studio, with its good northern exposure, on the second floor. It wasn't as untidy as the one at the lake, but it smelled the same, and B.J. wondered if all women found the mingled scents of paint and turpentine and man as erotic as she did—or just those who knew Cal.

One wall was all glass, angling up to form half the roof as well, and outside she could see lights of other houses far up the side of Hollyburn Mountain. Back in the huge living room, she looked out over the lights of the city with the black strip of Burrard Inlet separating shores joined by the arc of Lions Gate Bridge. In the kitchen, she met the tall, reed-thin Miss Lutz, whose smile transformed her face from stern to jovial, and felt reassured that the girls would be happy there. Miss Lutz lived in, and was pleased to have someone to see to. She was lonely, she said, with Mr. Mixall spending so much time in that awful place where the mosquitoes could carry off chickens. She had been there once and that had been plenty, thank you very much.

"Tuva's mom's going to pick us up and deliver us back home," Laura said when they dropped the girls off at the nearest McDonald's. "You guys don't have to worry about us. Just get on with your courting."

B.J. burst out laughing. "Laura, that's not what we're doing! Where do you get these ideas, anyway?"

The two girls just grinned impishly and ran to meet their friends. Cal grinned and slid an arm around B.J.'s shoulder, pulling her close. "She got the idea from me." He dipped his head and dropped a quick kiss onto her nose. "That's why we came back to town. I'm here to court you, B.J. So get used to the idea."

It was, B.J. discovered in the days that followed, an idea she took to quite readily. "I hope you know what you're doing," she said to Cal a couple of weeks later as they stood in the glass cage of the gondola lift to the top of Grouse Mountain. There was no snow yet, but the sky ride operated year round for the sake of the view and Cal was determined to go up. She clung to his hand. Beneath her feet, treetops whipped by with breathtaking speed, and the parking lot grew smaller and smaller until the cars looked like toys. Shutting her eyes tightly, she buried her face against his shoulder. "Are you courting me, or are you courting danger?"

"Don't be such a baby. This isn't dangerous. Don't you ski?"

She lifted amazed eyes to his. "Heavens, no!"

"Why not?"

Tucking her under his arm, he walked off the lift at the top. From the viewpoint they could see for miles over a vista of mountain and water and cityscape that defied description, but filled her heart with a sense of pride.

"Why didn't you ever learn to ski?" he asked. "I thought everybody out here did. You know, the Pacific Coast myth, golfing, skiing, and sailing in the same day with only twenty minutes separating each activity."

"It's no myth," she said. "But that doesn't mean everyone has to do all three, you know."

She thought about how she had once wanted to ski, but the desire had been brief, dying at the door of the sportswear store. One look inside had been enough to tell her that skiing was not for her. Nobody had ever asked her to go sailing, and though she'd tried golfing, it wasn't until recent years that she'd begun to enjoy it. Odd, she thought now. She hadn't even considered taking up skiing, as she had riding motorcycles, when it became physically possible. She decided she'd start thinking about it now, then she remembered that gondola ride. *Maybe* she'd consider skiing. Cross-country.

"How about you?" she asked Cal.

"I ski. I love it. I share time in a condo in Whistler. This winter, Ms. Gray, you are going to learn to ski."

Her eyes widened. "At *Whistler*? Not on a bet! As

you might have gathered on the way up here, I don't handle heights well."

"You handled the gondola ride beautifully," he said. "You look cute with your eyes squeezed shut and your knuckles all white. Besides, what if I promise to hold your hand all the way up, every time?"

She grinned and acquiesced. "Well . . . I'll think about it."

He stood silent for several moments, watching the wind play games with her hair, then lifted his hand from her shoulder to help the breeze along. He liked to see her hair tousled. It made him think of the way she was going to look in the painting.

What, he wondered, would she say if she knew how well it was progressing? More to the point, what would she say if she even knew he had started it without her permission? He shouldn't be doing it, he knew, without her knowledge, but he was compelled and could no more have stopped painting than Canute could have stopped the tide. Even the sick feeling of guilt he got when he really allowed himself to think about what he was doing couldn't force him to stop. She'd forgive him when she saw it. She would!

Bending, he kissed her hard and slowly, almost, she thought, desperately.

"Let's have lunch," he said when he released her.

She held back, her hand on his cheek, staring into his eyes. She was aware of his hand trembling slightly at the small of her back. "Cal? Is something wrong?"

He shook his head, but refused to meet her eyes until they were seated in the restaurant looking out over a different panoramic view. By then, his gaze was clear and his face relaxed, and as they talked, laughing together, enjoying each other's company, she forgot her worries, concentrating only on having a good time with Cal.

He told her about his childhood, and she laughed at some of the scrapes he'd got into. "You must have had a lot of fun," she said with unconscious wistfulness.

"Sure. That's what childhood is supposed to be all about, isn't it?"

She nodded.

"Hey," he said, frowning. "Tell me about yourself as a little girl. You had fun, didn't you?"

"Oh, yes." She managed a smile. She hadn't had the kind of fun he'd had, but it hadn't been all gloom, either. It was just difficult, sometimes, to recall the high spots.

"Oh, hell, B.J., I'm sorry," he said. "That was insensitive of me, wasn't it? You lost your parents when you were pretty young, didn't you? I guess things weren't so very wonderful for you."

"I was eight when they were killed," she said. "I scarcely remember them. Besides, I had Melody's parents, my sister Phyllis, and her husband Henry. They were wonderful and loved me—love me—as much as I do them. I didn't lack for anything.

"Melody and I both wished Phyllis and Henry had had more children. They may have wished the same; we never discussed it. But Mel and I used to pretend we were members of a huge family. We both had a wonderful time when my brother Edwin—he's the oldest—and his family used to come out from Edmonton for Easter every year. He and his wife have five children." She smiled in reminiscence. "That was a lot of fun. It's the only time that big old house was ever really crowded."

"Do you think you'll make it your permanent home again?"

She shrugged. "I don't know. It's a big place, as I said. It needs a family."

She felt Cal's gaze on her. "Don't you want a family?"

Oh, Lord, but she wanted one! The yearning for that was becoming stronger daily, but Cal seemed content for them to drift along, enjoying each other's company and letting their relationship develop without any haste at all. She shrugged and said, "Maybe. Someday." He let the subject drop.

If he'd been suggesting, she mused, that maybe she should start thinking about raising a family, he was being pretty subtle. In fact, she didn't even know if he wanted one, or if he intended this relationship of theirs to progress any further than the inevitable affair she was certain was going to happen very soon.

But how was it ever going to happen if he didn't make it happen? she wondered. Was she going to have to be the one to say the time was right? It seemed so, but she didn't know how. She wished she had the grace to do it with ease and finesse, to tell him with the heat of her kisses, the responses of her body, that she was tired of waiting. Though she tried, he always called a halt much too soon.

Words, a little voice inside her said. *Use the words, B.J. It's called communication.*

Theory was one thing, though. Putting such theories into practice was another, she discovered, feeling the words dry up on her time and again. Until the evening he asked her to show him what was happening in her house.

Nine

"There isn't much to see down here yet. Just this mess," she said, making a sweeping gesture to indicate the new, broad windows in the expanded living room. It had once been the parlor and den, which were now combined. The last rays of the sun angled through the streaked glass, picking up dust motes floating in air heavy with the scent of new lumber and glue. The kitchen looked as if an earthquake had shaken it up, tumbling its contents into a heap. A sawhorse blocked their way and they closed the door quickly on the scent of paint and putty.

"And that's about it," B.J. said. "Next week the wall between the old formal dining room and the library is coming out to make a family room, and the new dining room gets built when they push out the south wall of the kitchen. It'll be more interesting when it's all finished."

She drew in a shaky breath, her knees weak and her mouth dry as she added with false aplomb, "Want to see what they've done upstairs?"

Cal's breath stopped but he nodded casually. That was exactly what he wanted to see, what he'd hoped for in arriving early to pick her up for dinner and asking for this tour. Upstairs. The room where she had slept as a child. Her sanctuary from the world.

There, he hoped to find some of the missing pieces, the special nuances of growing up that had helped create the woman he knew now—yet didn't know well enough. If he could see the B.J. that had existed as a toddler, a child, a teenager, then maybe he'd be able to give his painting of her the depth he felt it was lacking. It was as if a secret portion of her was hiding somewhere, in spite of the honesty that had so attracted him at first. She was honest, he knew, but there were still sections of her life about which he knew nothing, as if she had drawn a veil, not of lies, but of omissions, over her childhood. He sensed there was so much more she could tell him, if only she would.

She pointed out the skylight at the top of the stairwell, opened the first door on the left, and showed Cal a big bathroom, whose claw-footed tub hadn't been replaced, only refinished, and another skylight set into a newly lowered ceiling. It was a far cry from what he remembered, and he saw the wisdom of the changes that had been made. The place had a friendlier feel about it. It was a home now, not so much a museum. He wondered if the antique furniture was to be replaced as well.

They peeked in at the girls' rooms, the master bedroom, and several others, all smelling of fresh paint and newly carpeted in the same pale beige as the hallway. None of the bedrooms had draperies to cover their enlarged windows, but the tracks had been installed. Opening another door, B.J. stood back for Cal to enter.

"This is my room."

He stepped in, finding it, as the others had been, large by modern standards, and airy, with pale peach walls, a big window open to catch the crisp October breeze, the sill wide enough for sitting. Outside, close enough to touch, the golden leaves of a huge old chestnut tree moved with a sibilant rustle. Within the room there was a double bed with a carved rosewood headboard, a matching dresser and chest of drawers, a chair, and a large closet covered by folding doors. He turned full circle and raised his brows. "This is it?"

"Yes."

"But where are the mementoes of your childhood?" He thought of his own room in his parents' home, the posters that still hung on the walls, the trophies in their case, the books he had loved, the pictures of himself and friends. Anyone looking at that room would know at once that while artistic, he'd also been athletic. They'd know that he liked adventure stories and science fiction and John Lennon and Jimi Hendrix.

"Where's the one frilly doll you couldn't bear to put away? The ribbons you won for spelling contests or footraces or whatever? Where are *you*?"

She smiled, understanding what he'd expected to see in her room. Opening the closet, she said, "In there. Packed away in boxes."

"Of course. You couldn't leave things out when the workers were in here." He put a hand on her shoulder, leaning down to look at the label on one of the boxes. "Photo albums. Will you show me?"

She froze, thinking of what his request could mean, and knew she could not show him. She shook her head. "No! I mean, not now. Maybe someday."

He turned her to face him, eyes dark as he stared at her. "Why not now? Today."

She pulled away quickly and bent. "Here," she said, reaching into the back of the closet and pulling out a smaller box. She set it on the bed. "I'll show you these."

"Report cards!" he said, sitting down on the edge

of the bed and opening the top one on the stack. "Hmm, smart little creature, weren't you? I didn't know they gave letter grades to six-year-olds."

"St. Agnes's did. It still does." She sat beside him, separated only by the small box. Her heart pounded hard in her chest. She felt unsettled, disturbed by being in her bedroom with him, on her bed, knowing that she wanted him, knowing that he wanted her and was only waiting for her to make some kind of move. Oh, Lord, would he still want her if he knew that the only reason she'd been holding back for the past weeks was because she didn't know how to tell him that she was ready? Couldn't he look at her and see that she was?

She ran a hand around the neckline of her sweater, finding it too tight, too warm. Did he really want to look at report cards, or was he only being polite, because she'd offered them to him? What would he do if she lay back on the bed, reached out her arms to him, and offered herself? She stared longingly at his profile, wanting to lean sideways and flick the tip of her tongue over the little curve at the corner of his mouth. A heavy heat seemed to be pressing down on her and making it difficult to breathe. Didn't he want what she wanted with increasing urgency? Oh, dammit, she knew he did, but knew that he had made her a promise he wouldn't break. Why did she have to fall in love each time with a man of such high integrity? she wondered. Not that she'd really ever been in love with Antonio, not like this.

She sighed silently and forced herself to relax.

Flipping through at random, Cal tried, through reading the teachers' comments, to form a picture of the girl B.J. had been. Whereas the remarks on his reports had been along the lines of *Talks too much in class* and *Spends more time doodling on his exercise books than doing his lessons*, B.J.'s teachers had considered her a model student. *Always completes her homework. Writes excellent English compositions.* Except for one teacher. Cal scrutinized the signature and saw that it was the same one for four straight years and that the comment seldom varied much.

He looked up at her and grinned, fanning out the pages showing that teacher's remarks. "I bet if this one had given you a motorcycle, you'd have put more effort into your physical education . . . 'Barbara.' "

She laughed huskily and with shaking hands stuffed the reports back into the box. "If they'd offered me a motorbike in those days, I'd have run away, scared stiff. I was not athletic."

Then what were you? Cal wanted to shout. He leaned across her to set the box on the bedside table, his arm brushing her breasts, and grimaced when she shrank away from his accidental touch. She got to her feet and would have left the room, but he reached out quickly and snatched her hand, spinning her around and drawing her close to stand between his legs. "When did you become B.J. instead of Barbara?"

She smiled, thinking of Melody's insistence that a new person deserved a new identity. "Mel started calling me that quite a few years ago. It seemed to stick."

"I'm glad," he said. "I like it. Are you ready to tell me yet what the J stands for?"

She shook her head. "You were supposed to come up with something to cover that."

"And I will. Someday." Then, frowning, he asked, "Why won't you show me the albums?" As her face tightened, he went on, "B.J., I only want to know you. Know the way you were, know the kind of child that grew into the beautiful woman you are. Is that so strange?"

She swallowed hard and stepped out of his reach. "Cal . . . I don't want to. Not today."

Getting to his feet, he encircled her waist with his arms. "When are you going to trust me?"

"I do trust you. It's just that we're . . . different."

He squeezed her gently as he drew her closer to his body, into the heat that emanated from him. "Not in any way that counts," he said quietly, his eyes burning into hers.

"In every way that counts," she argued. "You're so sure of yourself, Cal. And I'm not. I thought I was, but now I know I'm just as uncertain about things— about myself—as I used to be when . . ." She caught her lower lip between her teeth and dropped her lashes.

"No. Don't do that," he said sharply. "Look at me." He shook her gently and she looked up, still chewing her lip. "You think I'm sure of myself, but you're wrong. You scare me, B.J. I've never felt like this before, either, you know. For a long time I didn't know if I liked it, but in spite of that, I went with it because it feels so good I didn't want it to stop."

It shocked her to hear that he shared some of her uncertainties. Shocked, and somehow comforted her. What about her could possibly scare him? Was that why he was hesitating? Not because he thought she was afraid, but because he had a few doubts, too?

Emboldened by the idea that he wasn't as much in control as she had thought, that perhaps he needed almost as much encouragement as she did, she slid her hands up over his chest, letting her fingers curve around his shoulders.

"Do you like it now?" she asked. "The way you feel?"

Heat flared in his eyes as he pulled her against his chest. His hands stroked up and down her back, then cupped her buttocks and drew her into the cradle of his hips. Her fingers bit into his shoulders and she stared into his eyes, her own going slightly wild as he moved insinuatingly against her. To hell with caution, he said to himself. There had to be some way to communicate with her. If this was the way, then so be it.

"Doesn't it feel as if I like it?" he asked, his voice a low, tense growl. "Doesn't it feel as good and as right to you as it does to me?"

Desire surged within her. Tingling sensations slithered over her body, heating it, and she wanted those sensations to go on and on, build higher and higher, fly her to heights she could only imagine. "Oh, Cal," she murmured as she let her hands move around to the back of his neck, where her fingers locked. Pulling his head toward her, she placed her lips against his. "It feels very good," she whispered. "Make me feel . . . more."

Her soft admission and request undid him. He held her face in his hands as he angled his mouth across hers, kissing her with all the desperate need he wanted her to understand, and she arched up against him, moving her hips in a subtle rhythm that inflamed his already scorching body.

He felt the wild drumming of her heart. It was like something trying to escape from the cage of her ribs, and he knew that only part of it was excitement. She was afraid, too; he could taste it on her lips, feel it in her tremors. He let her control the kiss, loving the shy way she moved her mouth against his, the tentative exploration of her tongue over his lips and teeth, then the fluttering of it as she slipped it inside, where he sucked it gently. Her hands traveled down from his neck, onto his shoulders, over his powerfully muscled arms, then slid inside his suit coat, her fingers clinging to the back of his shirt, nails raking on the fabric. Slowly, almost furtively, she tugged on his shirt and put her hands under it, moving her palms softly over the skin of his back.

"It . . . feels . . . better than anything," she whispered, pressing against his hard body. Desire soared higher, and this time she succumbed to it without a fight. She wasn't afraid, she thought in amazement. She wasn't afraid of anything anymore!

Cal palmed one of her breasts, massaging slowly, and felt her flesh swell, grow warmer. Her soft murmurs of desire created a well of boiling pleasure in the pit of his stomach, and when her pelvis surged toward his, he slid his hand down to cup the throbbing center of her body, fingers moving slowly, evocatively, in small circles.

B.J. felt the strength of his hand, the curve of his fingers as he slipped them between her legs, and knew that she needed more than this, much more. With the same sudden flood of certainty, she accepted that this was the man, this was the time, and from here on, there could be no turning back. The barrier of their clothing could no longer be borne, and she broke the magic kiss as she reached up to undo his tie. Pulling it loose from his collar, she dropped it onto the dresser, then attacked the buttons on his shirt.

He nuzzled her neck, murmured in her ear, rocked her against him. Finally, when his shirt gaped open, she kissed his chest, loving the feel of his skin under her lips, the scent of it in her nose, the heavy pounding of his heart as it thundered in her ears. When an exploring finger found one of his hard nipples and she flicked it with a fingernail, he gasped.

"Honey, you'd better stop!"

She tilted her head back and sucked in a shuddering breath as she moved restlessly against him. "Do you want me to?"

His gaze questioned her, his eyes deep and dark.

His hand on her back trembled, and the other one rose to stroke her chin and throat. "No," he whispered.

"I don't want to stop, either," she said, her voice tremulous.

"B.J.?" Did she know what she was doing? Did she know what she was asking? Of course she did, he saw with a rush of joy. Her eyes were dark with passion and mystery, and her lips were parted, moist and swollen from his kisses, but there was a solid conviction in her gaze. She was ready for his love. "I didn't come here with this in mind," he said.

"I know." She could scarcely breathe. "But I did."

Still, he wanted confirmation. She saw him swallow hard as he loosened his hold on her. "But it only goes on from here if you truly want it to," he said, his voice husky with arousal.

She moistened her lips, then said so softly he wasn't sure he'd heard her, "I want it to. Don't stop. Cal, please. Make love to me."

"Oh, love!" His words trembled against her lips. "You'd better mean what you say because I've wanted you for so long that I won't be able to hold back."

"I mean it. And don't hold back," she murmured.

He felt the depth of her response, the strength of her conviction, as she caught his hand and brought it to her breast again, holding it there, moving it slowly as she cupped it around her fullness. He didn't need her encouragement. He caressed her willingly, thrilled and delighted in her womanliness and the pleasure she took in it.

He had known it would be like this. When B.J. wanted him, when she was ready to take this step with him, she would do so with all the ardor in her lovely soul. And he had known that she would be worth waiting for. She moaned softly, exciting him further, as he covered her mouth with his own and kissed her as he'd never dared kiss her before, with all of his heart and his love and his need unleashed, and it unlocked something in her as well, setting it free to soar.

It was a wild and willful kiss that took her by surprise, though it shouldn't have, B.J. thought, feeling Cal tremble as he snatched her even more tightly against him. His manhood rose hard and insistent against her, and he moved her slowly up and down along its length, groaning with pleasure. He filled her mouth with the hot probe of his tongue, thrusting inside, tasting, plunging with erotic demand in a seductive rhythm that her hips picked up and repeated. She tangled her hands in his hair, treasuring its crispness, the way it curled around her fingers, and taking sensuous pleasure in discovering the shape of his head, the muscles of his neck and shoulders. She could spend the rest of her days holding him, she thought, touching his body, breathing in his scent, hearing his breath and his heartbeat, feeling the taste of him on her tongue and lips.

She shoved at his jacket and he shrugged out of it, scarcely letting her go while he did so. His hands were hard on her back and buttocks, moving constantly as if trying to memorize her. As she arched again, pressing her pelvis against his, he lifted one hand and caught a hard nipple through the layers of her clothing. He squeezed it in little tugging pulses that she felt deep inside her. She gasped into his mouth, and he loosened his hold, but she parted from him just long enough to say, "That's so good. Don't stop!" then returned his kiss with her own exploring tongue.

He tugged at her sweater, but the belt around her middle held it down. He fumbled with the buckle, and the soft suede fell to the floor with hardly a sound. Then his hands were under her sweater, on the bare skin of her back, and she went rigid with the sensations that flooded her body.

"Cal . . . hurry!" she cried softly as he undid her

bra and slipped tiny buttons out of holes all down the front of her sweater. He tugged it off her, slid her straps down and away, then took both her breasts in his hands, stroking up from their undersides with a slow, reverent caress.

"So lovely," he said, looking from her full breasts with their hard, dark pink nipples and crinkled aureolas, into her eyes and then back again. "So perfect. I need to kiss them, B.J. I need to suck on them, fill my hands and my mouth with their sweetness, feel your nipples go hard against my tongue."

She made soft cooing sounds as he put his words to action. Her legs trembled, her head spun, and her breath came in short, agonized gasps as a feeling of helplessness overcame her, filling her with a hunger so powerful she thought it could never be filled.

"Someday," Cal said as he lifted his head, his voice and hands trembling, "someday you'll let me paint you like this, with your breasts all rosy and swollen, and their tips wet and hard from my kisses."

She couldn't speak, could only draw in a shuddering breath and stare into his eyes. *Anything, anything,* she told him silently. *Anything you want.*

He moved her backward until her legs touched the side of the bed, then he tilted her down, bending over her to kiss her breasts, kneeling astride her, his hair tumbling over his forehead to tickle her bare flesh, the open front of his shirt hanging down to make a private little tent for the two of them.

He lingered over each breast in turn, starting on the undersides, where the skin was so sensitive she nearly screamed with the teasing touch he gave her. The hot, hard tip of his tongue, the softness of his lips, the feathering of his breath and hair were driving her slowly to distraction. She shivered and scissored her legs against him as her whole body began to pulse deep within and her nipples tightened to nearly unbearable hardness. Clasping his head, she held him to her, moaning with need and pleasure.

His weight came down onto her, and her legs parted to make a secure place for him. Lifting against him, she murmured, "Please, please . . ."

"What do you want me to do?" he asked, his face buried between her breasts, his voice a vibrant tone she felt as much as heard. "What will make it the best for you it's ever been?"

"Cal, please, I ache so," she sobbed, but he only lifted himself on rigid arms and held her gaze, his eyes so dark with passion they appeared black. She saw herself reflected in them and thought how strange it was she had never seen herself that way before. It made her feel complete for the first time in her life, part of a circle, half of a pair, and she wondered if he felt the same, seeing himself in her eyes.

"What do you ache for?" he asked, flexing his body so that his hips rocked against hers. "What do you want? Tell me, love, so I can give it to you just the way you want it."

"I . . ." I can't, she had been about to say, but she knew she had to tell him, even though it would be the hardest thing she had ever done. But this was Cal, and he was going to make love to her—he was making love to her—and she was making love to him. So if she didn't say the words, maybe he wouldn't know how much she needed again what he'd just done, and she knew she would die if it didn't happen soon.

"Kiss me some more," she whispered, feeling heat rise up over her chest and her face, and praying he wouldn't notice that she was blushing like a schoolgirl. "On my nipples. Like you did before. Fill your hands and mouth with me."

"Oh, yes!" he said, then dipped his head to capture one hard nipple, pulling it fully into his mouth as his hand rubbed over its mate. She thought she would explode as she felt the tip of his tongue, hot and wet and rough, flicking at her nipple. Why hadn't she known it would be like this? Why hadn't she believed? Why had she waited so long?

"Like that?" he asked after a while, lifting his head and looking into her face. He saw joy and anguish and wonder all mingled together as she gasped for breath and stared at him, bemused. "Is that what you like, love?"

"I like it. Oh, yes!" She wanted to laugh. She wanted to cry. She did like it! She loved it! B.J. clung to his shoulders as her legs lifted and wrapped around his middle, drawing his hard shape closer, her entire body aflame with a kind of need she had never fully known before. And if she liked that . . .

"What else?" he asked, rolling to one side and sliding a hand down between her thighs, cupping the throbbing mound there once more, moving with her motions, complementing them until she thought she would melt, or fly away, or fall apart, or scream. . . .

"I think we have too many clothes on," she moaned, and he laughed against her neck.

"You're right, love. You're so right." He undid the button at her waist, slid her zipper down and then her pants, tugging them off until they fell from her ankles. "Lift up again," he said, his mouth on her quivering belly.

She shook her head. "You . . . have too much on, too."

"Not for long," he said. "But you come first. Then I can look at you while I undress. Lift."

He looked while he stood over her, dragging his shirt the rest of the way off and dropping it onto the floor. He looked as he slowly unsnapped his pants, just as slowly lowered the zipper, and B.J. felt herself go rosy all over under his avid gaze. She wanted to roll onto her side and hide herself. She wanted to cover her breasts with one arm and her lower body with the other hand. But even more than that, she wanted him to go on looking at her the way he was. And she wanted to see him.

"Take . . . them off," she said when he still hesitated, his clenched fists on the waistband of his pants.

He smiled and did as she asked, dragging down his underwear at the same time, then peeling off his socks in the same motion. He moved toward her and she held up a hand.

"No. Stay there." And as he had feasted his eyes, so did she. Slowly, she sat up and reached out a hand toward him, running it down his chest, over his stomach, her fingertips light as they traced the line of hair, explored his navel, feathered over the thicker, darker hair lower down, and then brushed over his rigid manhood.

He stiffened, just barely clinging to his control, but when her hand encircled his shaft, he groaned and joined her on the bed. His hand stroked over her breasts, then across her abdomen to cover the tight, curly hair between her legs as his mouth made little forays from her lips, to her throat, to her ear. Nibbling on her lobe, he whispered, "Tell me what else makes you feel good."

She moved under his hand, hoping that would indicate to him what she wanted. But he was waiting, his head lifted, looking at her, and her body was burning and there was no way out. Her laughter held something like tears, and she couldn't quite meet his gaze as she forced herself to say, "I don't know *how* to tell you. Or what to tell you. I'm great on theory, Cal, but damned short on practice. Just . . . just do . . . whatever you normally do at a time like this, but hurry!"

He hurried, all right, but he hurried away from her and sat up, drawing her up beside him as he stared down at her, his fingers biting into her shoulder. "What? What did you say?" He shook her, his breathing harsh in his chest, his eyes wild, his hair standing up from her fingers having run through it. "Are you telling me you're a *virgin*?"

"Is it a crime?" she flared, but her voice cracked with anguish, not anger. Cal groaned, pulling her close into his arms to rest his cheek on her hair.

"No, darling, of course it's not a crime," he said after several minutes had passed while he stroked her back, kissed her flushed face, letting the agony of unfulfilled desire slowly seep from both of them until their breathing was less labored.

"Then—why did you stop?" She laughed, a short, nearly tearful sound again.

He lifted her head and looked at her for a long time before he said quietly, "Because I love you, B.J."

She jerked back, staring at him. "*What?* What did you say?"

Holding her face in both hands, he looked into her eyes and smiled slowly. "I'm in love with you." He said it with such simple sincerity, she had to believe him. "I've been in love with you since you pulled your crash helmet off and fainted in my potato patch."

"Oh, Cal . . ." she said, and tears came to her eyes.

"Don't do that," he said softly, kissing her eyelids. "I don't ever want to make you cry." Reaching behind her, he grasped the edge of the spread and pulled it up around them both, wrapping them in a cocoon of warmth. "Why didn't you tell me, sweetheart?"

"Because I . . . didn't really know how. And I guess I'm a little bit ashamed of it."

"You shouldn't be. Nobody ever said there was a time limit on virginity." Rolling down onto the bed, he carried her with him, still wrapped together in the spread.

"We have dinner reservations," he murmured as her arms tightened around him and one of her legs slid between his.

Her eyes went wide. "You're not going to make love to me?" she asked. She slid her hands up and down over his bare chest.

"Not right now," he said, his voice thick.

She looked up at him. "I loved everything we did so far, Cal. I really want . . . the rest. Books, as you might know, just don't do an adequate job of . . . instructing."

She tried to laugh, but it was a weak attempt, and he felt the tremor in her fingers. His belly again clenched painfully with hunger for her, and he wanted to throw the cover aside and show her everything she wanted to know. And he wanted to take hours and hours doing it.

"I promise," he said solemnly, looking into her beseeching eyes, stroking her hair from her crown to her nape, "we're going to make love, B.J. Just . . . not right now." He kissed her ear, then her eyelids and her nose. God, how he loved her nose! "I didn't come prepared for this, B.J., and under the circumstances, I don't suppose you're protected."

She raised one hand and traced the outline of his mouth with a finger. "Do you mind? That I'm not . . . experienced?"

He didn't even have to think about it. "No. But I wonder how it can be. Can you tell me why? What stopped you? What made you not want to—until now?" He smiled gently and kissed her ear. "You aren't, as you've often pointed out, a child."

"And thirty-year-old virgins are about as thick on the ground as daisies in Death Valley. I can't explain it, Cal." She could have. She should have. But she wouldn't. Not today. Maybe not even tomorrow. She wished she could explain that terrible reluctance even to herself. She loved him. He loved her. Yet even with that miracle still singing in her blood, she couldn't tell him the truth about herself. There was, however, something she could do, would do, had to do.

"I don't want dinner," she said softly, running a tentative finger around one of his nipples. She felt his hardness increase against her thighs.

"B.J.," he said in a threatening growl. "We have . . . to have . . . dinner."

"Have me for dinner," she said.

He laughed. "Are you seducing me, Miss Gray?"

"Looks like it."

It felt like it, too, he decided, knowing he should put a stop to this right now. But it felt so good. Her hands moved over his body shyly, shaking slightly, yet growing ever bolder until she reached an absolute pinnacle of courage again and encircled him as she had earlier.

He groaned and snatched himself out of her hand. "Dammit, will you quit?" He tried to sit up, but he was tangled in her arms and legs and the heavy bedspread, to say nothing of his own desires, making him weak and unwilling to fight too hard.

"No." She walked her fingers down his back, onto his buttocks, and pinched him lightly. "I won't quit."

"B.J.," he said again, but with much less force. "I want to, love, but . . ." He forced himself to go on, forced himself to remember. ". . . no protection."

His breathing, she noted, was rough and ragged, and his hands were no longer trying to push her away. "I don't care," she said, nuzzling him from his neck to his nipples and all the way back up, seeking his lips.

"I do," he said. "Sweetheart, do you want to go to the altar pregnant?"

"No one gets pregnant the first time," she murmured.

He held her chin in his hand, grinning down at her. "If you believe that, I'm going to send away for Ann Landers's book about sex for the modern teenager."

"I'm not a teenager and I don't care if I go to the—" Abruptly, she shoved him away and sat up, her eyes wide. "Cal!" she said in a disbelieving voice. "Do you know what you just said?"

"I'm going to send away for—"

"No! Before. Altar?"

"Of course, altar. As in church. As in marriage ceremony. As in husband. And wife." Gently, he laid her back down and clasped her hands over her head with one of his while with the other he traced a line from her temple to her breasts.

"Wife?" she whispered. "Cal, I don't know the first thing about being a wife."

"You know as much about being a wife as I do about being a husband, but I'm willing to go for it if you are. Don't worry, darling. Experience isn't required. You're going to be the best wife a man could ever ask for." He bent and covered her mouth with his, gently, tenderly. "And I'm asking, B.J."

"Me?" she whispered, feeling joy mingle with terror and reluctance so that she didn't know which was uppermost or strongest.

"Of course you! I said I wanted to court you, didn't I? What else is the end result of a courtship, if not marriage?"

"I . . . never gave it much thought. I guess, to me, a courtship is just that. An entity in and of itself."

"Have I got news for you. A courtship, when I'm the courter and you're the courtee, leads only one place: the altar. Please, love? Marry me."

She couldn't speak around the tightness in her throat, and he seemed to take her silence for assent. She felt his big hands tremble as he held her tightly, his kisses roving over her face and neck and shoulders, until she finally captured his head and brought their mouths together.

"I love you," she finally managed to say. "Oh, Cal, I love you so much and I'm at the end of my cycle, so I'm pretty sure I'm safe and I think if I have to wait any longer I might explode, so please, please make love to me right now."

He laughed drunkenly and managed to untangle the spread, flinging it back and covering her with his body. "You bet," he said against her lips while his hands played lovely games down her sides. "Me too. And it isn't just 'might' explode. I'm gonna, and I'm going to do it deep inside you, B.J., where it feels the best."

"Yes," she said, twisting her legs around his. "Show me, Cal. And tell me, and teach me how to be what you need."

"You are what I need. Just you."

But he told her, too, and taught her, and showed her. As his whispered words became actions, she cried out and rolled with him, bringing aching, throbbing parts together, stroking as he instructed, making up little variations of her own that left him gasping as she gasped.

"Please, please," she heard herself begging. "Come into me now. Fill me like you said you would."

"Not yet. There's more."

"Oh, God, how can there be?" she asked, but then laughed in joy along with him when she heard herself add, "What? Show me, then."

She felt wild and voluptuous and wanton and wonderful. "Oh, yes!" she cried when he kissed her more intimately than she'd ever expected to be kissed. "Cal! I didn't know it would be like this!"

His hair was soft on the insides of her thighs and she rubbed against it, loving the sensations both there and where his tongue flicked. A great, rolling wave of something roared through her body, making her mind spin. She clutched at Cal's head so he lifted it, bringing himself back to her mouth, where she tasted herself on him.

"This is what I was meant for," she told him moments later, feeling the curled nest of his lower body hair tickling her lips and her nose as she nuzzled him. "Loving you."

"Don't . . ." he groaned, straining up toward her seeking mouth, wanting her intimate kiss even as he told her no. "Ah, love, stop now or . . ."

He snatched her away and rolled her onto her back. "Now!" he grated, and she parted her legs eagerly, feeling the hot, wet tip of him probing at her entrance.

"Yes! Now!"

She lifted sharply and took him into her in one strong motion. The explosions came instantly, and they were grand, and mutual, and one right after the other, until she lay trembling in his arms, gazing up at him.

"Well!" she said. "Oh!"

"Did I hurt you?"

"Hurt me?"

Still holding her, he rolled to one side, nestling her head on his chest. "I love you, B.J. With all my heart."

"Mmm," she said, and slept.

When she awoke, Cal was sitting in the chair, the bedside lamp turned on. He wore only his underwear and had one knee bent, the ankle resting on his other knee, a sheet of paper on a broken piece of plywood against his thigh, and a rapidly moving, stubby carpenter's pencil in his right hand.

Glancing up, he saw that her eyes were open. "Don't move any more than you can help, love," he said. "I've finally got you captured, the full beauty that's been eluding me all these weeks, you, golden and graceful—my golden swan. Smile at me and say, 'I love you, Cal.'"

Instead, she paled and snatched the cover up over her, eyes wide. "No!" she gasped. "Don't do that! Don't draw me, Cal. I told you you couldn't!"

He dropped the paper and pencil to the floor and came to her, sitting down, one hand on either side of her.

"B.J.? Why not, love?" He smiled, a smile that made her feel cherished and broke her heart at the same time. "You can't say we don't know each other well enough now."

"Oh, Cal . . ." *Tell him! Tell him!* shrieked a voice inside her. *Show him the albums. Do it now! Now, before it's too late!* "I'm sorry," she said in a tired voice. "I just don't want you to do it."

"All right, sweetheart. I'll never force you to do anything you don't want to do. But I can hope that someday you'll change your mind, can't I?"

She shook her head. "I . . . don't think so."

"Maybe I'll ask you again when we've been married for fifty years."

Panic bit into her. "Cal . . ." She sat up, clutching the cover to her breasts. "I didn't say . . . I mean . . ." God! How could she marry him when she couldn't even tell him the truth about herself? She buried her face in her hands, unable to look at him, wanting to hide. What would he think of her when he finally knew what a liar she was? What a fraud? He wouldn't only not want to paint her, he wouldn't want to marry her and . . .

"Hey, take it easy," he said, pulling her hands away from her face, enfolding her in his arms. "Am I moving too fast for you again, love?"

Relieved of the necessity to think, to make decisions at the moment, she slipped her arms around his bare torso and clung to him. "I do love you, Cal," she murmured against his chest. "I love you so very much!"

"That's all I need to know for now. For the rest, I can wait. Because, B.J., whether you're ready to admit it now or not, you and I have forever."

She nodded. "Yes. I think we do. I hope we do."

He heard the doubt in her voice and held her more tightly, wishing she could tell him what frightened her so much, but knowing that until she was ready, he couldn't press her for confidences.

She lifted her head some moments later and smiled at him. "Cal? Know something?"

"What's that?"

She lay back on the bed and held out her arms to him. "We also have all night."

Lowering himself beside her, he smiled slowly. "That's good," he whispered. "We're going to need it."

Ten

Despite her misgivings, B.J. found herself accepting the ring Cal wanted to put on her finger. She had never come right out and said she'd marry him, but since she'd never said she wouldn't, he assumed that they were definitely getting married. Not right away, of course, but in time. That, she learned, she could live with. As long as she knew there was time, time in which to find the courage to come clean, then the pressure to do it immediately was off her.

And if being courted had been wonderful, being engaged was the most stupendous thing that had ever befallen B.J. Cal's tenderness and attention left her feeling like a pampered princess, but never more than the night of their engagement party. When he'd first suggested it, she'd objected.

"We don't need that."

"Yes, we do. If we're going to wait to get married until Mel and Curt come home, then we'll have a big party so I can meet your friends and family and you can meet mine. I'm proud of you. I want to show you off."

"Nah," she'd said, wrinkling her nose and turning

her left hand from side to side so the candlelight caught in her diamond and sapphire ring. "You just want to show this off."

"That's right," he'd said. "I'm an inveterate show-off." Taking her hand, he'd drawn it under the table and onto his lap. "See?"

"Oh!" Her eyes had widened in surprise and delight. "Yes, siree, Mr. Mixall, you are indeed a show-off!" Leaning closer, she'd whispered, "And what, exactly, can you do with that . . . object?"

"Let me take you home, and I'll show you."

She'd pretended to consider his suggestion. "And what if I don't like what you show me?"

"Then I won't make you go through an engagement party. Deal?"

"Deal," she'd agreed, and now that the party was in full swing, she was glad all over again. To her great joy, Phyllis and Henry had taken time out of their bicycle tour of Australia to come to the party, and Edwin, the elder of her two brothers, had flown out from Edmonton with his wife Sylvia and three of their five grown children, each of whom had brought several offspring of their own as well as mates. Graham, her other brother, a handsome bachelor, had come "stag, as usual," as he put it, so he could dance with anyone he pleased.

"So why are you wasting time on your baby sister?" B.J. asked as he swung her around the floor.

"It's never a waste of time being with you, Sissy," he said, whirling her so the skirt of her blue dress flared out around her legs. He twirled her away, holding her only by one hand, then brought her back. "You're good to look at, little one. That man of yours is lucky."

"I'm the one who's lucky," she said. She'd panicked at first, thinking that some member of her family might refer to the old B.J. in front of Cal. Now, as the evening progressed, and no one seemed to remember that she hadn't always looked this way, she found herself wishing someone would disclose the secret she'd kept from Cal for too long. At least then it would be out in the open—and she'd know, one way or the other. "I . . . I can't really believe he loves me," she added, looking worriedly at Graham. "Or that he should."

"Of course he should, and I can see that he does, and that you love him. It's about time, I think. You've been single too long."

She laughed. "Look who's talking! I'm only thirty. You're fifty-six."

Graham looked pensive for a moment, then said, "You know, I once found someone I felt for the way your man feels about you, but I made a mistake and let her go. So you hang on to that love of yours, Sissy. Hang on to it tight. It's important."

She hugged him. "I know it is, and thank you."

Giving her a quick hug in return, her brother set her away from him. "I guess I figure somebody should talk to you like a father, and as a much older brother, it seemed to be my duty."

Next it was Edwin's turn. Over a drink in a quiet corner, he scowled down at her. "You're happy, aren't you?"

"Very happy, Ed."

"He's good to you?"

"Wonderfully so."

"Well, he's ever anything but, you come to me. I'll sort him out in a hurry."

"Thanks, Eddie. You're a good brother."

"Well, I wasn't always. I was the oldest, and when our parents died, I should have taken you in, given you a home, raised you myself. But I didn't. And I always felt I'd done wrong."

"Ed, there's no need for feeling like that. I was better off in my own home, a familiar place, and

Phyllis and Henry loved me as if I were their own. They were wonderful foster parents. I wasn't unhappy."

His scowl deepened. "But you could have been a lot happier. I never figured out why Phyllis let you stay so . . ."

"Fat," she supplied. "A psychologist told me that Mom and Dad probably overfed me as an infant and a small child to compensate for not having wanted me. When Phyllis and Henry took over, they let me go on overeating because I was a sad and bereaved little girl and food seemed to comfort me. By the time anyone realized exactly what was happening, it was too late and I was busy engineering my own destruction. You can't blame yourself or anyone else. It was just the luck of the draw. And now my luck has turned, and I am happy, Eddie. Happier than I ever believed possible."

"Excuse me, Edwin," said Cal, lifting B.J.'s untouched drink out of her hand and putting it on the tray of a passing waiter. "May I have my fiancée for a few minutes? I miss her when she's away too long."

"Take her, son. Take her. With my blessing." Edwin raised his glass in salute.

Cal gathered her close and they danced away. "I'm glad I have somebody's blessing," he said with a chuckle. "Henry just told me that he's the nearest thing to a father you have, and that he felt it was his place to tell me that you weren't as sophisticated as some of the women I might have known, and to be patient with you. The suggestion was that if I didn't make you happy, he was going to rip me into small pieces, or words to that effect."

B.J. laughed. "Wow! From having no father, I seem to have gone to having three of them all in one evening. Graham's just been handing out advice to me, and before you came and rescued me, Ed was threatening to sort you out on my behalf if you didn't treat me nice."

"I'll treat you nice," he said, and she shivered at the promise in his tone.

"When?" she asked. She rubbed the tips of her fingers around the back of his collar, sliding them onto his nape and into his hair. "You haven't treated me nice since this afternoon."

He looked down at her, his eyes slumberous and full of love. "If you don't cut that out right now, Miss Gray, you might find yourself missing your own engagement party."

She smiled at him. "We wouldn't want that to happen, would we?"

His hand traced the low V at the back of her dress and slipped inside the silk fabric, finding living silk much more to its liking. "Oh, wouldn't we just!"

"Yeah," she said. "We would, but we'd disappoint a whole lot of people, I guess."

"Who'd you rather disappoint, me or a bunch of strangers?"

"I won't disappoint you," she said, and cringed inside, thinking that eventually she was going to have to do just that. But not tonight. No. Tonight was too special to ruin with confessions that should have been made long ago.

"I know you won't. You never have. You never will. I love you, B.J."

He drew her closer and they danced in silence, content for the moment just to hold each other, love each other, breathe in each other's scents. When their guests had finally gone, Cal surprised her with the key to a suite he'd taken in the hotel where the party had been held.

"So we don't have to waste time driving home," he said. They went up to their room and neither was disappointed in the other.

"I hate dropping you off here," Cal said on the

Monday morning following their party. "Do you know
how empty my bed is while you're tucked away in
your virginal little boarding-school bed? How lonely
my heart?"

"No more lonely than mine," she said, holding his
hand. As they had every other Monday morning since
the school had reopened in early November, they
were trying to say good-bye discreetly in full view of
a school full of girls—interested, nosy girls. At least
B.J. wanted to be discreet. Cal had no such intention.

"But you have a classroom of active kids to keep
you occupied," he said, tugging on her hand. She
slid a few inches closer. Just close enough to feel the
warmth of his body, she promised herself. Just close
enough to smell the scent of his skin.

"You have your work," she said. "And a show coming up in less than two weeks."

"I know. Are you sure you have that weekend free?
I can't do it without you, B.J."

"I'm sure I have it free. And even if I didn't, you
could do it without me. You have many times before."

"That was then. Now, I need you."

"You've got me. But you also have to let me go."

"Kiss me."

"Cal! Those girls will giggle and I'll blush, so don't!"

"I like to see you blush," he said, and gave a tug
on her hand, tumbling her across the seat and into
his arms. "Kiss me," he said against her lips. She
gave in, opening her mouth under his, accepting
the deep, loving caress of his tongue and returning
it in kind.

When she opened the door and stepped out of the
car, Kara came running to take her hand. "B.J.—I
mean, Miss Gray," she whispered, "you're blushing."

Cal leaned out his window and called, "I love you,
Miss Gray!" The girls giggled. B.J. blushed even
brighter, and turned to wave as he drove away.

"How was the party?" Kara asked. "And how come

you didn't come for breakfast with us yesterday like Grandma and Grandpa did? Are you going out for dinner with us tonight? They got special permission to take us out because they're going back to Australia tomorrow so they can finish their bike tour."

"Kara," said her sister. "Give her a chance to tell us about the party. The first bell's going to go any minute!"

"Hi, Laura," B.J. said, hugging her other great-niece. "The party was wonderful and I'll tell you all the details later. I wish you could have been there."

"Me too, but Grandma says when it's the wedding reception and we're bridesmaids, we get to stay as long as we want."

"Right, and now I have to run or my students will get to class before I do." She kissed them both and darted away, skirt swinging around her knees.

That was *her* wedding reception they were talking about. Each time she thought of it, she got butterflies in her stomach, and they weren't always the pleasant ones of delightful anticipation. Did all brides feel like this even months before the wedding, or was it her increasingly guilty conscience bothering her?

As the days passed B.J. grew more and more disappointed in herself for her continued silence and the way it was affecting her relationship with Cal. But was it just her secret, as she suspected, raising a cloudy barrier between the two of them? It could be, she knew, partly his concern and nervousness over his coming exhibition. And with that on his mind, how could she justify easing her own by adding another burden to his load?

She told herself she was using his exhibit as an excuse, but as it seemed like such a good one, she let her silence continue. She knew he was excited. There was a quiet tension about him that almost hummed sometimes, and as the opening night of his show grew closer, he grew more and more anxious. By the time that Friday itself arrived, he was unable to eat dinner, unable to sit still, unable to talk. He paced, his face taut and white, glancing at his watch over and over again, rubbing his face with one hand as if wiping away sweat.

"It's going to be all right," B.J. told him, sliding her arms around him. "Everything's perfect. Lord, are you always like this before a show?"

"No."

"So what's different this time?"

"I—I can't talk right now."

He jerked out of her arms and strode away, leaning on the window of his studio, looking up the mountain at lights that blurred before his eyes.

Oh, hell! he thought. He wanted to tell her. He needed to tell her. He should tell her. He should have told her weeks ago. He should have showed her weeks ago. But he hadn't, he couldn't, and now it was too late, because if he told her now and she hated the idea, she might refuse to go. If she didn't go, she wouldn't see it, and if she didn't see it, she wouldn't be able to understand. And what if she hated him for what he'd done?

She wouldn't! Of course she wouldn't. Phyllis, her own sister, who was as close to her as a mother, had told him that. "She'll be thrilled," Phyllis had said, and hugged him. "I wish I could be here to see her face when she sees it, Cal. You're right to keep it as a surprise. If you tell her, she'll just fret and spend her days and nights on edge wondering if anyone else will like it. As of course they will. I wish you'd reconsider selling it, and let us have it. Living over in Victoria, we don't get to see her often enough, and you'll have the real thing."

"It's not for sale, Phyllis. Not for any amount," he'd said. Right now, though, he'd give it away for nothing, if only he didn't have to go through any more of this self-imposed agony of wondering if he was doing the right thing.

"Darling, it's time to go," B.J. said, coming up behind him and placing a hand in the middle of his back.

He wheeled and crushed her in his arms, oblivious to the fact that he was also crushing her cream silk dress and the pale gold and pink orchid he had pinned on her not fifteen minutes before. "I love you!" he cried, kissing her with a desperation she could only wonder at. "Don't ever forget that. I love you more than I love anything else, or anyone else in the entire world!"

"I know, love," she said, gently disentangling herself. "I'm not going to forget it."

He was silent as they rode in the back of the limousine the gallery had sent, silent as they pulled up to the brightly lighted forecourt where a milling group swirled and separated, some going inside, others waiting, microphones poised, alert, watching for the guest of honor.

When Cal opened his door, he was immediately surrounded. When B.J. stepped out with the chauffeur's assistance, another group isolated her, shouting questions at her.

"Ms. Gray, do you have any words for us as you go inside to see this very special exhibit? Is this a big moment in your life?"

"Yes, of course. This is the first of my fiancé's shows I've ever attended."

"But the portrait, Ms. Gray, the portrait. How do you feel about that?"

B.J. blinked in consternation at the man who had asked. "What portrait?"

"The one we're all waiting to see. Surely you have, even if no else has, not even the gallery staff."

"I'm sorry. I think there's some kind of mistake. My fiancé doesn't—"

"Haven't you seen it yourself?" asked someone else.

"No. I don't know what you mean. My fiancé doesn't paint portraits."

"Then what about the one that's to be unveiled tonight? It's listed here as Mr. Mixall's first portrait." A reporter waved a printed sheet at her. "Model, Miss Barbara Gray. Don't you feel honored to be the subject of a painting entitled *Enchantment*?"

"Is it a nude, Ms. Gray?" asked a woman in bright red.

"Is that how you met your fiancé, Ms. Gray? Were you one of his models?"

A dull roaring sound filled her head. She tried to answer the question, but when she opened her mouth, no words came out. She closed it again, hearing again the words, *Is it a nude, Ms. Gray?* and hearing Cal saying, as he had that night so many weeks ago, *Someday you'll let me paint you like this, with your breasts all rosy and swollen, their tips wet and hard from my kisses.*

"No . . ." It was a soft moan of protest, heard by no one but her. He couldn't have! He couldn't have taken something so personal, so private, so precious as their love and the way it made her look, the way she had thought she looked only for him, and put it on public display! Could he? She looked at him over the top of the limo, her eyes wild with panic, and he gave her a helpless smile, a shrug, as if to say, "What can I tell you?" She let out a tearing cry and wrenched open the door of the limousine just as it started to edge out through the crowds. She tumbled inside, slamming and locking the door behind her.

"Miss? Miss?" She heard the driver, but couldn't lift her head to look at him. Humiliation filled her. Pain radiated from her every pore. *I've finally got you captured, the full beauty that's been eluding me all these weeks. . . . Smile at me and say, "I love you, Cal."*

And she had snatched the covers up and told him to stop.

But though he may have stopped drawing, he had sneaked away and painted. Painted her.

"Take me home," she cried. "Please, please, get me out of here!" Dimly, she heard a pounding, but still didn't lift her head. The locked door shook, but she was oblivious.

"Miss, Mr. Mixall's running after us," the driver said.

"Just keep going! Go!" she moaned, and huddled there as the big car turned the corner and the sound of shouting was left behind.

Sometime, she must have given the driver her address, because she found herself handing him her keys so he could unlock the front door. "Will you be all right, miss? Should I call someone? A friend? A doctor?"

"No. Thank you. Good night."

She closed the door and sank to the floor, wishing for the release of tears. There were none, only a burning, aching emptiness that went right to the bottom of her soul.

At length she arose and went to her room, opened her closet, and took out an album. She sat on the edge of her bed and stared at the unopened book. She didn't need to open it to see what was there, and because she had never showed Cal, he didn't know. What he had done was her fault. Because of her, he had made a complete fool of himself in public. He had used his talent to perpetrate a lie, and once he knew, he would never forgive her.

When she heard the door open downstairs, she knew it was him, but was too heartsick to get up and close and lock the door to her bedroom, or even to tell him to go away. Besides, what good would it do? He wouldn't go. Not until he knew the truth. And once he did, he'd go, and then maybe she'd be able to cry and rid herself of this terrible ache in her chest.

"B.J." He stopped in the doorway, looking at her narrow back, her bent head. "Why did you run? You could have let me explain."

She didn't turn. "You shouldn't be here. You have a show to open. A . . . portrait to unveil."

"To hell with that!" He strode into her room, stopped in front of her. "Don't you understand? Without you, without the portrait, there is no show! And that portrait won't be unveiled unless you're there to do it."

She lifted her head and looked at him. "Good," she said softly. "Then it won't be unveiled. At least you'll be spared that humiliation."

He crouched before her, not touching her, but looking at her ravaged face. He'd expected tears. What he found was a hundred times worse. Tears filled his own eyes and he blinked them back. "I didn't mean to humiliate you. I did it because I love you. Because I want you to see yourself as I see you. It was the only way I could show you, B.J. The only way to convince you of the truth. I know you don't think you're beautiful, and I wanted you to see that you are."

She let out a long breath and shook her head. "I said *you'll* be spared the humiliation, Cal. Not me. Oh, I admit at first that's all I thought about, but sitting here . . . with this"—she patted the leather cover of the album—"I realized that I had done something terrible to you, and that in doing it—not doing it, rather—I might have cost you your career."

"What? Darling, what are you talking about? Make sense, B.J. I know you're upset because I didn't tell you about the painting, but if you give me a chance, I'll try to explain."

She shook her head. "No. You don't need to explain. I do. Cal, you have a reputation to uphold.

You have a wonderful future ahead of you. You're the 'realism' painter. You show the soul of everything you paint. You show the truth. And if you painted me beautiful, it's because you don't know the truth." She patted the bed beside her. "Sit here. Let me show you . . . realism."

With a shaking hand, she opened the album on her lap, and Cal looked down at the first picture. It was a studio portrait of a chubby baby with curly blond hair. *Janie*, said the caption underneath.

"Cute baby," he said, wondering where this was leading, but knowing he had to let her do it her way. She was strained as taut as a piano wire; the least little touch and she'd break.

She nodded and turned page after page.

The snapshots were all of the same baby as she grew to be able to sit alone, then stand, and finally walk. Still chubby, she was pictured in various poses and with various adults or other children. The little girl who appeared with her in most of them was Melody, Cal realized. His sister-in-law hadn't changed drastically, and the resemblance to both Kara and Laura was marked.

But it was the pictures of the child named Janie his gaze lingered over. He saw with a pang the point in her life when Christmases and birthdays were no longer shared with parents, but with an older sister and her family. He watched the pale hair darken and straighten as the years were marked by turning of pages, and watched the chubbiness turn to blatant fat, then outright obesity.

B.J., who had avoided these albums for years, felt sick as she watched the progression from cute little girl, round with baby fat, to enormous schoolgirl with braces on her teeth. Eventually, the family snapshots became fewer and fewer until there were none, only one head-and-shoulders photograph on each page, marking each year of high school.

She wanted to slam the album shut and crawl under the bed, but she sat there stoically, looking with Cal at the repulsive, big-nosed teenager who refused to smile because of those braces. With each year's picture, the ugliness grew along with the nose. Dull, greasy, lank brown hair hung over the straining shoulders of a school uniform when she was fourteen, and the first of a crop of pimples was beginning to show. The hair was shorter in the next school photo, curled, but just as dull, and the face was even rounder, more dotted with acne, and the nose had developed a distinct hook and begun to appear wider at the tip.

In the picture taken when she was sixteen, there was a glimmer of a smile, because the braces were gone, but it seemed to emphasize the large nose and the acne that even the most careful airbrushing couldn't completely eradicate.

Cal felt her shivering beside him and put a warm arm around her.

No, he kept thinking. This can't be B.J. How could she, with her slender body, her wonderful skin and brilliant eyes, have come out of such a chrysalis? But he had to believe her. She had no reason to lie, and he understood now why he hadn't recognized her as the girl he had met twelve years before. Of course he hadn't. It may have been the same person, but it wasn't the same body, or even the same face.

After the page that held her graduation picture, she slammed the book and got to her feet, pacing away from him.

"B.J. . . . ." he said quietly. "Barbara Jane. Janie."

"You got it," she said harshly. "Janie. How's that for exotic. Remember, you wanted me to have an exotic middle name? All part of the illusion, I guess. And now do you see why I hate it when you call me beautiful? When you talk about my blue eyes? My pretty little nose? When you go on about my 'purity of soul,' my 'lack of artifice'?

"I am nothing but artifice! Under this false skin, I'm the original Plain Jane. The one the family called Sissy, or Janie, because she was named for her beautiful mother, and Barbara, or Barbie, couldn't be used for someone who was so horribly unlike the original!"

"Whoever said that to you?" His expression said he'd like to commit mayhem on them.

"Nobody ever said it, but I knew, and I was Janie to everyone except at school. My school had a policy then of no nicknames, so they called me Barbara. Now do you remember the girl who entertained you the weekend of Curt and Melody's wedding? The one with the funny eyes? The fat one? The ugly one? The girl you laughed at, Cal!"

"B.J.!" He strode to her and took her by the arms. He didn't understand anything, not her anger, or her pain, or why he seemed to be at fault. "What do you mean, I laughed at you? I don't know what you're talking about!"

"Then I'll tell you," she said, dry-eyed but anguished as she wrenched herself free from him. "I was just like that—" She went back to the bed, flipped open the album, and held up her high-school graduation picture for him to see. "Three hundred and two pounds, Cal! They had to have a special gown made for me. The others girls joked that they'd ordered it from Jones Tent and Awning! Maybe they did. I don't know. But that's what I weighed that summer, the summer I met you." She flung the album down in disgust.

"I don't know why you don't remember me. I can't have been all that forgettable, with pustulating acne and that awful, ugly, obscene beak of a nose!" She sobbed once, a dry, harsh sound, then regained control and faced him again, her eyes enormous, her skin without color, even her lips bloodless.

"And you know what?" she said disbelievingly. "You were nice to me! That's what made it all hurt so much. I really thought you liked me. You'd treated me like a real girl. We'd laughed together while I showed you around town. We liked the same music, the same movies, the same fashions—not that I could ever have worn anything even remotely fashionable, but I still knew what I liked—and we shared enough common beliefs that we could talk together for hours. And did. You were the first man who'd ever really listened to anything I'd said, or tried to explain anything about himself to me. And we danced together. I didn't know how, but you showed me that it was easy. And fun, and that was the first time since I was a child that I'd really had any fun. It hurt so bad, Cal, when it all came crashing down and I knew that you weren't my friend, that you didn't really like me, that I was an object of ridicule even to you."

"I do remember you, B.J.," he said quietly. "I remember that girl. Janie. One green eye, one gray. Funny, I remember her as being overweight, but I don't recall a really ugly nose. And she—you—were nice to me, too, when I was so down I could have slipped under the carpet and never even get tripped over."

She covered her face with her hands. "If you liked me, why did you laugh?" Her moan of pain cut into him like a dull knife.

"Darling, I don't remember laughing at you." He took her hands down and cradled her face. "I don't remember thinking of you as an object of ridicule. Honestly." When she only continued to look at him like an injured child trying to be brave, he said softly, "Tell me what happened."

She swallowed and blinked back tears. "It was at the reception. One of the ushers—I guess he was a friend of yours and Curt's—asked if you were expecting a flood. You asked what he meant and he said because of the way you'd been dancing all evening with that big orange life raft. And then you laughed. I was standing on the other side of the screen that had been set up to keep the buffet separate from the dancing, and I heard you. You know, of course, which side of that screen I was standing on," she added bitterly.

Her voice cracked and she turned to stare out the window at the chestnut true turned black in the dusk.

He remembered her awful orange dress, but not the comment he'd laughed at. But still . . . "I'm sorry I laughed."

"You laughed very loudly."

"Oh . . . hell!" he cursed softly, then she felt his arms come around her from behind. "If you say I did, then I must have. But B.J., maybe it was one of those reflex laughs. I don't find what that guy said funny at all now. Maybe I wasn't even paying attention. I really was pretty self absorbed back then." He was silent for a few minutes, swaying from side to side as he tried to comfort her, to ease a twelve-year-old hurt that could probably never be erased from her bruised psyche. But he loved her and he had hurt her, however unwittingly, and he had to try.

"Remember when we were playing that game with the kids up at the lake, and you drew the card about laughing at an ethnic joke? Do you remember what you finally had to choose as your answer?"

Slowly, she nodded, and he felt the tension beginning to seep out of her. She sighed. "Okay. Maybe that did happen to you. I guess it's all part of the insecurities I had from back then. I mean, it happened so long ago."

"Is that the reason you told Laura and Kara you didn't like me?"

"Yes. I'd put you out of my mind for a long time. The memory was too painful. Then when Melody

asked me to be coguardian with you, I had to remember. When she asked me to go up to Kinikinik
Lake, I refused because I thought you'd recognize
me and make me feel . . . bad about myself again."

He rested his chin on top of her head and rubbed
his hands up and down her folded arms. "And did
I?"

She shook her head. "You know you didn't. You
didn't even remember me."

He looked at her reflection in the window, then
turned her, her back still to him, and placed her in
front of the mirror. "Do you wonder why?"

"No." She managed a weak smile into the grave-
ness of his reflected eyes. "I know how much I've
changed outwardly. It cost me a lot in money and
pain and time. When I was twenty-one, I came into
my inheritance from my parents and that's the way I
spent some of it after I returned from South America. So you see, I am a creature of artifice. What you
see is not what you get. What you see is the result of
rhinoplasty and breast-reduction surgery, dermabra-
sion and a weight-loss program that took more than
four years to complete. To say nothing of colored
contact lenses. Even my dimples are the result of a
surgical procedure. I had one deep, pitted scar, so
the surgeon gave me a matched set."

She turned and faced him. "So, artist, what do
you think now?" she asked, her voice ragged and
hoarse and defiant again. "Still want to show the
world a painting of the beautiful, totally honest,
good-from-the-inside-out woman?"

"Yes."

She stared at him. "*Yes?* Cal, didn't you hear a
word I've said? I'm a fake. A construct! A product
of modern science! I am not real!"

"You *are* real. You're a warm, caring person. And
you worked hard and suffered to become as beautiful outside as you were inside. Snatching up the

album, he opened it at random. "Is that real?" He pointed to the baby depicted there. "This?" He opened to a page showing her as a ten-year-old. "Do those pictures look the same? Of course not, but they represent the same person, B.J., just as this does." He turned her around to face the mirror. "How can you see one image as more 'real' than the other? They simply show different stages of development. Do you think I won't love you when you have a seamed face and white hair?"

She felt tears rise up along with hope, and crushed both back down. "Look at me," she said, turning from the mirror. "I dye my hair!"

He laughed. "So do I."

She gaped at him. "What?"

"It's true. I started going gray when I was only twenty-nine, and I hated it. Made me look old. So I use that stuff that you comb in. It works. I feel lots better about myself when I look good."

She drew in a tremulous breath and laughed. "You must feel great about yourself, then."

"And so should you, my darling. You're Barbara Jane Gray, B.J., a very special lady to me, whether you call yourself Janie or Barbara or B.J. I love you, and I painted you because you are not only beautiful on the outside, you are beautiful on the inside, where it counts."

She looked at him and felt the pain ease out of her chest as the tears welled up in her eyes. They overflowed even as he tried to wipe them away with his hands. "I love you," she said. "I'm sorry I ruined your opening by running like that."

"That doesn't matter. I was wrong for not telling you about the portrait. I wanted to, but I was afraid. I thought if you saw it too soon you'd worry about it, about how it would be received. But everyone is going to love it, darling. Because it is a very beautiful image of a very beautiful woman. So will you come back to the gallery with me? Will you unveil it for me?"

Her tears flooded over again. "Cal, I love you, but I can't do that even for you. I'm sorry. Oh, please try to understand. To me, the way I look for you is just for you. If I have to unveil it and let everyone there see what my body looks like when you're making love to me, it will demean our love. It won't be special anymore. Please, Cal, don't ask me to do that and—"

"Wait a minute!" He shook her gently, his dark brows pulled together. "What do you mean, what your body looks like when we're making love? Dammit, B.J., have you got some weird idea that I painted a nude of you?"

"Well, yes."

He shook her again, a little harder. "Well, you just happen to be wrong! You've got some lousy opinion of me if you think I'd share with anyone, especially the public, what goes on between us in the privacy of our bedroom." Snatching up a tissue from the box on her dresser, he carefully dried her eyes. "B.J., I promise that portrait isn't something you need to be ashamed of, or something that will embarrass you in any way." She hesitated, her mouth trembling, and he kissed her gently. "Please, sweetheart? Trust me."

And wasn't that, after all, what loving him was all about? What she should have done long ago? Swallowing hard, she nodded. "Okay. I trust you."

"Cal . . . I'm really nervous," she whispered, clinging to his hand, her other hand on the gold cord she was about to pull. The canvas stood on a pedestal, its top two feet over her head. Life-size, it was billed, and a hushed crowd waited for its unveiling.

"Don't be," he murmured. "The painting is good,

love. The best I've ever done. And if it doesn't convince you of how totally lovely you really are, I'm just going to have to spend the rest of my life trying to do it some other way. Now pull the cord. Everyone's waiting."

B.J. pulled. The gold drapes parted, fell away, and she stepped back with Cal, staring. Tears filled her eyes and her whole body began to shake. She struggled to control herself as she looked at his work of art, his portrait from the heart, recognized the love in every brush stroke.

Perched astride her bike, she was dressed in black leather, with a V of pink sweater showing at the front. Her gauntleted hands gripped the handlebars, her helmet sat on the ground near the toe of one boot, and she was smiling, dimples dancing. Her hair, caught by the morning sun, lifted by the breeze, shimmered and seemed to move.

"You see?" Cal said quietly. "What is that, an ugly duckling or a golden swan?"

As applause began and grew, B.J. turned to Cal. He caught her in his arms and gazed into her eyes. "Well?" he asked. "Are you convinced?"

Her dimples flashed as she laughed impishly. "Nope. So have you got a lifetime to waste trying to convince me?"

Right there, in front of the applauding crowd, he kissed her long and hard. "You bet," he said fervently.

And B.J. blushed.

THE EDITOR'S CORNER

1990. A new decade. I suspect that most of us who are involved in romance publishing will remember the 1980s as "the romance decade." During the past ten years we have seen a momentous change as Americans jumped into the romance business and developed the talent and expertise to publish short, contemporary American love stories. Previously the only romances of this type had come from British and Australian authors through the Canadian company, Harlequin Enterprises. That lonely giant, or monopoly, was first challenged in the early 1980s when Dell published Ecstasy romances under Vivien Stephens's direction; by Simon and Schuster, which established Silhouette romances (now owned by Harlequin); and by Berkley/Jove, which supported my brainchild, Second Chance at Love. After getting that line off to a fine start, I came to Bantam.

The times had grown turbulent by the middle of the decade. But an industry had been born. Editors who liked and understood romance had been found and trained. Enormous numbers of writers had been discovered and were flocking to workshops and seminars sponsored by the brand-new Romance Writers of America to acquire or polish their skills.

LOVESWEPT was launched with six romances in May 1983. And I am extremely proud of all the wonderful authors who've been with us through these seven years and who have never left the fold, no matter the inducements to do so. I'm just as proud of the LOVESWEPT staff. There's been very little turnover—Susann Brailey, Nita Taublib, and Elizabeth Barrett have been on board all along; Carrie Feron and Tom Kleh have been here a year and two years, respectively. I'm also delighted by you, our readers, who have so wholeheartedly endorsed every innovation we've dared to make—our authors publishing under their real names and including pictures and autobiographies in their books, and the Fan of the Month feature, which puts the spotlight on a person who represents many of our readers. And of course I thank you for all your kind words about the Editor's Corner.

Now, starting this new decade, we find there wasn't enough growth in the audience for romances and/or there was too much being published, so that most American publishers have left the arena. It is only big Harlequin and little LOVESWEPT. Despite our small size, we are as vigorous and hearty, excited and exuberant now as we were in the beginning. I can't wait to see what the next ten years bring. What LOVESWEPT innova-

(continued)

tions do you imagine I might be summarizing in the Editor's Corner as we head into the new *century*?

But now to turn from musings about the year 2000 to the very real pleasures of next month!

Let Iris Johansen take you on one of her most thrilling, exciting journeys to Sedikhan, read **NOTORIOUS**, LOVESWEPT #378. It didn't matter to Sabin Wyatt that the jury had acquitted gorgeous actress Mallory Thane of his stepbrother's murder. She had become his obsession. He cleverly gets her to Sedikhan and confronts her with a demand that she tell him the truth about her marriage. When she does, he refuses to believe her story. He will believe only what he can feel: primitive, consuming desire for Mallory. . . . Convinced that Mallory returns his passion, Sabin takes her in fiery and unforgettable moments. That's only the beginning of **NOTORIOUS**, which undoubtedly is going onto my list of all-time favorites from Iris. I bet you, too, will label this romance a keeper.

Here comes another of Gail Douglas's fabulous romances about the sisters, *The Dreamweavers*, whose stories never fail to enmesh me and hold me spellbound. In LOVESWEPT #379, **SOPHISTICATED LADY**, we meet the incredible jazz pianist Pete Cochrane. When he looks up from the keyboard into Lisa Sinclair's eyes, he is captivated by the exquisite honey-blonde. He begins to play Ellington's "Sophisticated Lady," and Ann is stunned by the potent appeal of this musical James Bond. These two vagabonds have a rocky road to love that we think you'll relish every step of the way.

What a delight to welcome back Jan Hudson with her LOVESWEPT #380, **ALWAYS FRIDAY**. Full of fun and laced with fire, **ALWAYS FRIDAY** introduces us to handsome executive Daniel Friday and darling Tess Cameron. From the very first, Tess knows that there's no one better to unstarch Dan's collars and teach him to cut loose from his workaholism. Dan fears he can't protect his free-spirited and sexy Tess from disappointment. It's a glorious set of problems these two confront and solve.

Next, in Peggy Webb's **VALLEY OF FIRE**, LOVESWEPT #381, you are going to meet a dangerous man. A very dangerous and exciting man. I'd be surprised if you didn't find Rick McGill, the best private investigator in Tupelo, Mississippi, the stuff that the larger-than-life Sam Spades are made of with a little Valentino thrown in. Martha Ann Riley summons all her courage to dare to play Bacall to Rick's Bogart. She wants to find her sister's gambler husband . . . and turns out to be Rick's

(continued)

perfect companion for a sizzling night in a cave, a wicked romp through Las Vegas. Wildly attracted, Martha Ann thinks Rick is the most irresistible scoundrel she's ever met . . . and the most untrustworthy! Don't miss **VALLEY OF FIRE!** It's fantastic.

Glenna McReynolds gives us her most ambitious and thrilling romance to date in LOVESWEPT #382, **DATELINE: KYDD AND RIOS.** Nobody knew more about getting into trouble than Nikki Kydd, but that talent had made her perfect at finding stories for Josh Rios, the daring photojournalist who'd built his career reporting the battles and betrayals of San Simeon's dictatorship. After three years as partners, when he could resist her no longer, he ordered Nikki back to the States—but in the warm, dark tropical night he couldn't let her go . . . without teaching the green-eyed witch her power as a woman. She'd vanished with the dawn rather than obey Josh's command to leave, but now, a year later, Nikki needs him back . . . to fulfill a desperate bargain.

What a treat you can expect from Fayrene Preston next month—the launch book of her marvelous quartet about the people who live and work in a fabulous house, SwanSea Place. Here in LOVESWEPT #383, *SwanSea Place:* **THE LEGACY,** Caitlin Deverell had been born in SwanSea, the magnificent family home on the wild, windswept coast of Maine, and now she was restoring its splendor to open it as a luxury resort. When Nico DiFrenza asked her to let him stay for a few days, caution demanded she refuse the mysterious visitor's request—but his spellbinding charm made that impossible! So begins a riveting tale full of the unique charm Fayrene can so wonderfully invent for us.

Altogether a spectacular start to the new decade with great LOVESWEPT reading.

Warm good wishes,

Carolyn Nichols

Carolyn Nichols
Editor
LOVESWEPT
Bantam Books
666 Fifth Avenue
New York, NY 10103

FAN OF THE MONTH

Hazel Parker

Twelve years ago my husband Hoke insisted that I quit my job as a data processor to open a paperback bookstore. The reason was that our book bill had become as large as our grocery bill. Today I am still in the book business, in a much larger store, still reading and selling my favorite romance novels.

My most popular authors are of course writing for what I consider to be the number one romance series—LOVESWEPT. One of the all-time favorites is Kay Hooper. Her books appeal to readers because of her sense of humor and unique characters (for instance, Pepper in **PEPPER'S WAY**). And few authors can write better books than Iris Johansen's **THE TRUST-WORTHY REDHEAD** or Fayrene Preston's **FOR THE LOVE OF SAMI.** When the three authors get together (as they did for the Delaney series), you have *dynamite*. Keep up the good work, LOVESWEPT.

60 Minutes to a Better, More Beautiful You!

Now it's easier than ever to awaken your sensuality, stay slim forever—even make yourself irresistible. With Bantam's bestselling subliminal audio tapes, you're only 60 minutes away from a better, more beautiful you!

__	45004-2	**Slim Forever**	$8.95
__	45112-X	**Awaken Your Sensuality**	$7.95
__	45081-6	**You're Irresistible**	$7.95
__	45035-2	**Stop Smoking Forever**	$8.95
__	45130-8	**Develop Your Intuition**	$7.95
__	45022-0	**Positively Change Your Life**	$8.95
__	45154-5	**Get What You Want**	$7.95
__	45041-7	**Stress Free Forever**	$7.95
__	45106-5	**Get a Good Night's Sleep**	$7.95
__	45094-8	**Improve Your Concentration**	$7.95
__	45172-3	**Develop A Perfect Memory**	$8.95

THE DELANEY DYNASTY

Men and women whose loves an passions are so glorious
it takes many great romance novels by three bestselling
authors to tell their tempestuous stories.

THE SHAMROCK TRINITY

THE LATEST IN BOOKS
AND AUDIO CASSETTES

Paperbacks ————————————————————

☐ 27032 **FIRST BORN** Doris Mortman $4.95

☐ 27283 **BRAZEN VIRTUE** Nora Roberts $3.95

☐ 25891 **THE TWO MRS. GRENVILLES**
Dominick Dunne $4.95

☐ 27891 **PEOPLE LIKE US** Dominick Dunne $4.95

☐ 27260 **WILD SWAN** Celeste De Blasis $4.95

☐ 25692 **SWAN'S CHANCE** Celeste De Blasis $4.50

☐ 26543 **ACT OF WILL**
Barbara Taylor Bradford $5.95

☐ 27790 **A WOMAN OF SUBSTANCE**
Barbara Taylor Bradford $5.95

Audio ————————————————————————

☐ **THE SHELL SEEKERS** by Rosamunde Pilcher
Performance by Lynn Redgrave
180 Mins. Double Cassette 48183-9 $14.95

☐ **THE NAKED HEART** by Jacqueline Briskin
Performance by Stockard Channing
180 Mins. Double Cassette 45169-3 $14.95

☐ **COLD SASSY TREE** by Olive Ann Burns
Performance by Richard Thomas
180 Mins. Double Cassette 45166-9 $14.95

☐ **PEOPLE LIKE US** by Dominick Dunne
Performance by Len Cariou
180 Mins. Double Cassette 45164-2 $14.95

— — — — — — — — — — — — — — — — — —

Bantam Books, Dept. FBS, 414 East Golf Road, Des Plaines, IL 60016

Please send me the items I have checked above. I am enclosing $_____
(please add $2.00 to cover postage and handling). Send check or money
order, no cash or C.O.D.s please.

Mr/Ms _____

Address _____

City/State _____ Zip _____

Please allow four to six weeks for delivery.
Prices and availability subject to change without notice.